His kiss had made that obvious. Yet he was not coming back. He wouldn't return, she was sure, despite the powerful attraction they shared. She knew he would be steeling himself against this love he had not bargained for, a love that had popped into his monastic life like a jack-in-the-box.

And it had been the same for her. She hadn't expected anything like this to show up on *her* packed agenda.

Yet, here indeed was a man to whom she *could* commit for a lifetime.

Was the *"Pere éternel,"* the "Eternal Father" who Nick honored so completely, working behind the scenes, calling such strange plays as briefcase exchanges for Nick and herself?

It seemed that might be true.

She fell back against the wall, pressing her fingers to her eyes. "Oh, God, on the chance that You're out there listening, I appeal to You. You know how much that sensational man deserves joy and happiness in his life. I pray—yes, Lord, I *do* pray—that if You've chosen me to be the agent of his happiness, You will show me how to bring it about."

She brushed her hair back from her face, her tears drying salty against her cheeks, as she remembered to add, "in Jesus' name."

GINGER O'NEIL is thrilled with the publication of her first novel. She lives in Virginia with her retired Air Force lieutenant colonel husband. They have six grown children and several grandchildren. Music and writing have played a large part in her life, so she has combined those loves in *A Touching Performance*.

A Touching Performance

Ginger O'Neil

Heartsong Presents

A note from the author:
I love to hear from my readers! You may correspond with me by writing:　　　　**Ginger O'Neil**
Author Relations
PO Box 719
Uhrichsville, OH 44683

ISBN 1-57748-755-9

A TOUCHING PERFORMANCE

Cover illustration by Ron Hall.

PRINTED IN THE U.S.A.

one

A grotesque, mangled face flashed onto the thirty-nine-inch screen. Black strings of hair framed the mask, with blood from scalp wounds pooling around still-staring eyes before streaking down into the contorted mouth of the victim.

Twenty-seven-year-old Claire Rossiter allowed herself only a fleeting glance. A reluctant and bewildered participant in the proceedings, she squirmed in her chair to the left of the eight other witnesses in the Fulton Falls courtroom.

She'd seen accident victims on the television news often enough, but never had she beheld a visage so disfigured as the one before her now.

On the witness stand a nervous, elderly man answered the endless questions of a persistent prosecutor.

That witness actually had seen the accident happen. Claire had not.

How foolish it seemed to have to report to a hearing in this backwater village when she hardly qualified as a witness at all—her car was the ninth in the ten-car chain of minor collisions resulting from the fatal crash.

The only pertinent information she could provide dealt with weather and the road condition. She hadn't a shred of evidence suggesting that the death of the female victim resulted from a hit-and-run, or that it was purposeful killing inflicted with Mafia-style *malicious intent*. Malicious intent?

How could it be? she thought to herself as she clenched and unclenched her fingers. *What kind of human being would create such carnage intentionally and then drive away?*

Never, as far back as Claire could remember, had "malicious intent" been part of her world, a world dominated by music—both in childhood under the guidance of doting parents and teachers and in her late teens and early twenties as she performed in concerts organized by supportive conductors and agents.

Astonishing success had recently arrived for Claire after she won the celebrated East Coast Schumann Piano competition. However, to her great dismay, that award, plus the ten-city concert tour it guaranteed, had come six years too late for her adorable papa to share. He'd gone—almost eagerly, it had seemed—to a heavenly reunion with his wife, Claire's whisper-soft mother whom he'd lost fifteen years earlier.

A sense of obligation to the litigants forced Claire to steal another glimpse at the video that was grinding out ever more hideous angles of the corpse.

Death here screamed out at her with sickening viciousness, whereas death in her own family had been nothing more than quiet relinquishment—Mozart melodies in church escorting a soul to eternity.

She ran her long fingers through scales and cadences on the arm of her chair until, quite accidentally, her fifth finger tapped a C-sharp onto the arm of the woman next to her. Claire offered a sheepish, "Oh, I'm so sorry."

The highly rouged, red-haired woman smiled back. "No problem." With a shrug of a shoulder she whispered a husky, "This is the pits."

The heady perfume of the woman's bouffant hair assailed Claire, who seldom used hair spray—or any cosmetics at all. Most of the time, a puff or two of face powder on her cheeks and the application of a lustrous, rose-colored lipstick was enough.

Claire knew she didn't need much in the way of artificial enhancement. Over the years, her appearance had seemed to please the most critical audiences, both those attending her performances and those among her closest associates at State University, where she taught.

Her long, lean bone structure of face and body appeared fragile. "A deception," her teacher in Switzerland had declared.

Madame Bouchard had compared Claire to a stained-glass window. "Exquisitely lucent, yet skillfully crafted to withstand stress."

She smiled, remembering.

Interrupting the attorney in midsentence, the judge pounded his gavel, announcing a fifteen-minute recess, the first of the morning. According to the printed schedule, Claire noted that she'd be the next witness to be called. A good thing; she definitely had to get to New York by midafternoon for a few hours of practice.

The lawyers had rescheduled her. They knew about her well-publicized recital the next evening at Lincoln Center.

"Boy, could I go for a strong cappuccino," announced the red-haired woman, her chair squeaking as she stood up. "How 'bout you, dearie?"

Claire offered the woman a relieved grin. "That sounds ideal right now."

"There's a snack bar downstairs," added the woman. "Why don't we check it out?"

"Great." Claire thrust legal papers into her briefcase on top of her music, picked up her purse, and followed the woman out of the courtroom.

Because the mobbed snack bar had only a few tables, most of the patrons drank their coffee and munched bagels standing up, shoulder to shoulder. A shelf by the doorway held a pile of miscellaneous briefcases and portfolios. Claire put hers there and lined up for coffee with the other woman.

She scanned the packed room. All manner of conversations buffeted her ears. To her right, a group of women were denouncing a sex-education course being taught at the local high school. To her left, two farmers were discussing the best feed for hogs. And in the background she could hear voices debating a zoning ordinance dealing with a sanitary landfill.

It had been a long time since she'd considered the necessity for sanitary landfills—or high school sex education. Maybe that wasn't a good thing. Living in an ivory tower of music had its drawbacks.

Standing above his companions in a group near the tables was a tall man who appeared as out of place in the surroundings as she assumed herself to be. *He's more suited to a tennis court than a courthouse,* Claire told herself, pleased with her private play on words.

What is the exact color of his hair? Claire pondered. She decided it was a toss-up between corn silk and Dijon mustard. An unlikely combination, yes. But on him it looked tremendous.

Because his hair had a casual going-every-which-way-at-once style, at first glance someone might think he'd let a frivolous girlfriend go at it with a pair of rusty scissors, but Claire knew otherwise. That effect—tousled and carefree—required the hands of a skilled stylist who knew what he was doing.

Errant strands, permitting no semblance of a part, went into free-fall across the young man's high, bronzed forehead; at the moment, his eyes were squinting in merriment over some comment made by one of the four men standing with him.

The "What'll it be, ladies?" from across the counter prompted Claire to place her order.

Fortunately, a table became vacant almost immediately. The redhead maneuvered through the crowd to grab it.

"This coffee's a lifesaver," said the woman. "I had to get off work to come up here today. Boy, that kills. I'm a waitress in the city, see. I lose a couple hundred bucks in tips on days off."

"It's been inconvenient for me, too," Claire added, finding the woman's conversation a refreshing change from the deliberations in the courtroom.

"What kind of work do you do?"

"Most of the time, I teach," Claire answered, realizing she might make the woman uncomfortable if she admitted she was a concert pianist, her teaching duties secondary in importance.

Even as she tried to be cordial with her companion, Claire couldn't prevent her eyes from analyzing the tall blond man.

The chest-high part of his tan suit, which was about all she could see, was well tailored. A striped tie lay loose below his collar, establishing an understated flair, almost as if he'd put it on, already knotted, over his head.

He stood tall with his hands behind his back, like members of the British royal family. His companions, none quite so smartly turned out or as young as he, were all prosperously clothed gentlemen. Though they did most of the talking, the tall man seemed to be the leader of the group—not due to his height, but, rather, because he had the demeanor of one who was in charge.

"What do you teach?" the redhead asked.

Trying desperately to be polite to the woman, Claire smiled as she replied, "Piano and keyboard at the state university."

"Well, whadda you know! Say, we have a terrific piano player where I work. He can play anything. My favorite's 'Come Back to Sorrento.' Can you play that?"

Claire grinned good-naturedly. "Yes, I've run through that a few times."

To Claire's delight, the tall man's group was being pushed closer to the table where she and the redhead sat.

Claire studied the sharply delineated jaw of the blond man. His chin barely missed being too long; it had been clipped by nature just in time. But "nature," or what more accurately should be described as the Divine Sculptor, had bestowed on him full, expressive lips, which he now pressed tightly together as he listened to the other men.

She figured he must be about thirty-eight. And she was willing to bet he boasted a Dutch or Nordic heritage.

"You're so pretty," the redhead stated. "You should play in a club, yourself. You've got *gorgeous* black hair. I bet you can twist it up real elegant-like."

Claire nodded, shifting so she could see the woman and the tall blond man at the same time. "Sometimes I do wear a chignon," she offered.

"Hey, put a little more eye shadow on and find yourself a

slinky gown. You'd be a sensation. This piano player at our place could get you into a club in the city. He knows everybody."

Claire laughed. "I might consider it."

"If you get sick of teachin', come on in. You meet swell people in restaurants and clubs. I like my work a lot. The hours aren't bad and. . ."

The woman's comments now competed with the conversation of the blond man's group—that group discussing prisoners and paroles, subjects both startling and fascinating to Claire.

"Zimblatz deserves to be paroled," said a squat man in a brown suit. "I'm not going to stand here and let you convince me otherwise, Nick. Everettsville's bursting at its seams. Even with the new facility, you're going to be crowded. Zimblatz has played by the rules for fifteen years. He deserves his walking pap rs."

"I'm sorry, Ed, I don't agree," replied the tall man, shaking his head, a look of regret on his face. Claire was delighted with the name Nick. She decided it suited him perfectly.

"Granted, Frankie Zimblatz has been an industrious mechanic over the years," the Nick-guy continued. "He's kept the engine purring on my chariot; I can't fault him on that score."

"So, Nick, that proves he's responsible," said another man in the group.

"His record looks pretty good on the surface," Nick said, shrugging a shoulder and lowering his head to one side, causing strands of hair to fall a different way. "It's been a year since he's been involved with drugs or had a fight, but there are things that don't get entered on the record. His expression, his way of looking at you, tells me he doesn't have his life together yet."

Nick paused. The other men appeared impatient as they waited for him to continue.

Despite his opposition to the prisoner's parole, there didn't appear to be any severity in his startlingly blue eyes, recessed under soft, straw-colored brows.

The red-haired woman cleared her throat. ". . .So you can see how great it is where I work. It kills me to lose all those tips."

Claire feigned interest, barely hearing what the woman was saying as she tried to juggle the two conversations, the woman's job losing ground to the Zimblatz parole.

"I've seen Zimblatz's hostility a thousand times in other men," Nick continued, "and it always tells me they're not ready. Zimblatz hasn't worked things out inside, down in his spirit, where it counts. I know this sounds unscientific, but—"

"Unscientific! It's downright medieval, and you know it," countered the man in the brown suit. "What kind of malarkey are you handing us, Nick? Who among us ever has everything worked out down inside 'where it counts,' as you say. Do you?"

"I like to think so, yes. But it didn't come easy."

"No, I guess not," the man responded, rubbing his chin, "especially in your case. But some of us, for whatever reason, don't share your belief in things of the spirit—things like God or eternal life or whatever. I don't happen to think a man has to nail himself to a cross or declare himself saved over a loudspeaker to be given a parole."

Nick responded quickly, with some irritation, "Ed, you know me well enough to realize I never let a prisoner's religion or lack of same influence my recommendations to a parole board. I've been scrupulous about this."

He lowered his eyelids reflectively as he continued. "But I'll readily admit I think these guys under my charge would benefit enormously if God became a part of their lives."

Claire was struck by the intensity of his words as he went on. "To go back out on the streets after ten, twenty years behind bars and face the complexities and prejudices of an unsympathetic environment is a monumental task. Without God as the sidelines coach, it's virtually a no-win situation. But never have I required religious allegiance in a parole approval."

"He's right," a man with a black mustache stated in acquiescence. "We've all dealt with Nick enough to know that's true."

"Thanks, Len." Nick's mouth formed a smile. "In Frankie

Zimblatz's case I'm doing society *and* Frankie a favor, keeping him incarcerated."

"You're still a sadist in my book," the brown-suited man chortled. "If you had your way, you'd turn thumbscrews and go back to the lockstep."

"Give me a break," Nick said with a scowl, retaining the telltale smile lines in his cheeks. "Ed, I've recommended plenty of paroles for you these past four years since I've been at Everettsville. Only last month, I pushed hard for the release of Sam Baker and Clyde Randolph, hardly saints in either case. I'm just telling you, your buddy Zimblatz isn't going to make it. He has three murders to his credit. Would you like to make it four? If you and the board release him, it's your ball game entirely. I won't sign an endorsement."

One of the men offered to get coffee for the others. Nick said a barely audible, "No, thanks." Claire noted he was the only one in the group who didn't already have a cup or a snack in his hand.

He's a health freak, Claire thought. *No caffeine and no cholesterol.*

The red-haired woman cleared her throat. ". . .So you see how great it is where I work. Drop in sometime. It's the Ravenna Lounge off Washington Square. Just ask for me— Emma. I'll see that you get yourself a thick Omaha steak."

"I'm sure you would, ah, er, Emma," Claire managed with a smile, wondering if the tall blond man would ever blow his healthy regimen and order himself a thick Omaha steak in the woman's bistro.

"Those inmates must hate your guts," said the mustached man. "Nick, there's probably a contract out on you."

"I'm sure there's more than one," Nick replied, amusement fading slowly from his smile.

Contracts?

Claire shuddered at the very word, all lightheartedness vanishing from her thoughts. Nick-the-warden had just admitted there likely were contracts out on him, apparently not at all unusual in his line of work.

"Actually," said the man named Ed, "it amazes me, Len, but Nick has an excellent rapport with most of the inmates at Everettsville."

"Except at parole time," joked Len.

"Yeah, except at parole time," echoed the other.

Claire was startled to see the red-haired woman getting up to go.

". . .So, really," said the woman, who had continued her conversation unheeded, "I think it's time for us to get back."

"You're right," replied a startled Claire, looking at her watch. She was reluctant to leave because she'd developed a deep curiosity about the fate of the unfortunate Zimblatz.

More than that, she was captivated by this Nick person, who apparently held some sort of major position in a penitentiary.

He didn't fit the picture she would draw of a prison warden, not that she'd spent an inordinate amount of time over the years trying to envision such a person. In every respect, the man appeared too East Hampton sophisticated for a role of that type.

She couldn't imagine him ever shouting at squads of men, ordering them over catwalks or back into cages.

But more than anything else, his Christian witness astonished her. It seemed inconsistent, somehow, for this tennis-buff kind of man to acknowledge so confidently his dependence on God.

Claire considered herself a responsible Christian, often accompanying choruses and performances in churches of many denominations, as well as her own. On Sundays she regularly attended church services. But her day-to-day prayer time had become slipshod. It had been ages since she'd prayed for God's direction in her life.

As a child, she'd prayed every night with her father. Before bedtime there'd be a story, usually in French, and then a little chat, also in French, with *le Père éternel*.

But as she grew beyond childhood, piano practice had taken

up more and more time. Talking to "the Eternal Father" had been relegated to the background of her life. After her father's death, she'd let her daily prayer time slip away with him.

In more recent years, she'd more or less assumed ministers and the university philosophy department were handling things like that for her. Music was enough for *her* to handle. More than enough. Mastery of any one field didn't permit spreading oneself too thin.

Yet there were moments in music—such as after the sustained echoes of a perfect cadenza in Franck or the interlacing of a Bach fugue—when she was transcended to an all-encompassing ecstasy that couldn't be explained by harmony, the science of acoustics, or just her basic love of music.

There'd been that afternoon last year in Westminster Abbey when she'd heard the *Laudamus Te* of Haydn's Lord Nelson Mass. That simple, yet so ethereal, selection had stunned her with its majesty. She'd left the abbey shaken by what could only be described as the awesome presence of God, a God who needed more of her than she was giving Him.

In a similar way, Nick's strong statements had unnerved her. She hadn't expected to be so emotionally stirred in this environment.

The red-haired woman headed into the group of corrections personnel. "How's about letting us get outta here, fellas?" she quipped as she edged her way around the man named Ed.

Feeling like a quarterback following a center tackle, Claire stayed close to the other woman. "Excuse us," she mumbled to the men, unable to prevent her eyes from searching out the expression of the rivetingly handsome Nick.

His eyes, like chips from a blue glacier, returned her glance in a way that forced her knees to buckle a little, hampering maneuverability for a second.

"Show your manners, men; let the ladies through," Nick announced with exaggerated command, as he stepped back into the crowd of farmers behind him. "Although we don't show much prison know-how, allowing two such gorgeous creatures to escape so easily," he added.

He permitted a smirk to take over his puckish lips.

Claire couldn't help but laughingly reply in a similar dramatic tone as she shouldered a path to the door. "Thank you, kind sirs, for providing us safe passage."

He's probably married, with at least five children and a harried wife, she thought as she picked up her briefcase from the shelf. *Maybe his wife and children march lockstep to their beds.* She snickered as she contemplated this scene.

Buoyed into a more cheerful frame of mind by the roguish Nick, she headed back to the courtroom.

But, she reminded herself, *Nick was roguish only up to a point.* His comments and mannerisms indicated he was well aware of the power he wielded over prisoners and their paroles. He was anything but frivolous in his approach to his job.

With his drollery, his captivating eyes, and his expressive lips, Nick dominated her mind as she stepped into her place next to the other witnesses.

How she wished she'd been able to listen to him longer. His conversation certainly had more going for it than the dismal dirge of the accident hearing. In fact, his conversation was more interesting than most she was a party to back at the university.

She and the redhead had no more than gotten comfortable in their seats when the judge announced the lawyers had come to a settlement in the case. The remaining witnesses wouldn't be needed. He thanked them and told them they were free to leave.

Claire looked at her watch. Only 11:37. She'd have plenty of practice time that afternoon, after all.

She turned to the red-haired woman, and they both shook their heads.

"That beats all," said the waitress. "I take this whole crummy day to drive up here, and they never even ask me to get up on the stand. Man, this has been murder! I bet you're as mad as I am."

"It's exasperating, but chalk it up as an experience. For me, it's been an education," Claire admitted.

"For me, it's been a bummer," stormed the woman. "So, see you around. Remember now, the Ravenna Lounge. If you ever need a job, come on in."

"Thank you," said Claire, touched by the woman's sincere concern. "You never know. Right now things are going pretty well for me. But if I *do* need a job I'll look you up."

"Right. So long." The red-haired woman pushed her chair back and strutted from the room.

Claire got up slowly. For the waitress, this day had been a "bummer." By all accounts, it should have been a bummer for her, as well. But it hadn't been. Listening to Nick talk with his colleagues about paroles had made it more than worth the inconvenience.

As she started down the path toward her car, she weighed Nick's comments. There was something so steadfast and rock-bottom-reliable about Nick's manner that she was convinced his actions would never be frivolous or petty.

It made her feel secure and almost cozy as she drove down the highway to the city, knowing that a man named Nick carefully screened the prisoners he released back into society.

two

Claire took no time for lunch when she got to New York, but went directly to Lincoln Center for her practice session.

Tossing off her jacket, she spun through a series of arpeggios and exercises. To her disappointment, the third-octave G had poor action. She'd have to mention that to the tuner in the morning.

She flipped open her briefcase to check the time the tuner was expected. To her bewilderment, her briefcase held nothing familiar. No jottings about the accident. No subpoena. No folder of music. No program. Nothing of hers.

Who was playing tricks on her?

Closing the case, she examined the cover. It looked exactly like hers. The handles were the same. But it *wasn't* hers! The black leather had a slightly different grain.

There were black initials near the handle—N.S.V. Immediately her mind registered N for Nick. Might this briefcase belong to the attractive warden of Everettsville Prison? *It might very well,* she reasoned, *because the mix-up could only have happened in the snack bar at the courthouse.* She'd grabbed the wrong case from the shelf.

"Good grief," she groaned. "If this is his briefcase, I've done a terrible thing to that guy."

Once again she opened the briefcase. It was imperative she find out for sure who the owner was. She'd have to phone the courthouse right away—try to get in touch with the owner before he or she left for the day. Whoever it was had already been without notes now for most of the afternoon.

Her own inconvenience paled in comparison. She didn't really need her music; she'd had everything committed to memory for months. Only the program and some memos

17

would have come in handy. But it was discomforting to realize she'd inconvenienced someone else to the extent that crucial decisions might have been made haphazardly—in situations like that of the prisoner Zimblatz.

What a careless, stupid thing she'd done.

She thumbed through the brochures and magazines that lay in the briefcase. They all dealt with prisons. There was a pamphlet on juvenile recidivism, a manual on penal codes, several corrections periodicals. She felt almost criminal herself, pawing through someone else's material. But it was necessary. Unless she found a name written somewhere, she couldn't be sure the briefcase belonged to Nick. Maybe it was the property of a person named Nelson, Neil—even Nancy or. . .

Then she saw it. The full name and address on a magazine. And it *was* Nick—Nicklaus S. Van Vierssen. How many Nicks in a rural courthouse would have a briefcase filled with material on prisons and penology? It had to be the tall blond man.

Nicklaus Van Vierssen. So very Dutch. It was the ideal name for him. She could almost see him standing on a sluice gate, wearing a white cable-knit sweater, and looking out over a canal, his hair whipped into a frenzy by a North Sea blast.

But she mustn't squander time in daydreams. She had to phone the courthouse right away and report what had happened.

As soon as possible, she had to drive back to Fulton Falls with the briefcase.

Dinner with Henri would have to be canceled.

Removing her cell phone from her purse, she located the number for the county clerk's office in Fulton Falls. That would do. They could locate Nick Van Vierssen, if he hadn't gone home. But certainly if he *had* gone, he'd have left word with someone that his briefcase was missing.

Thank heaven her recital wasn't scheduled for that evening. But she'd still have to phone Henri and tell him she couldn't make their dinner engagement. Or maybe Henri would drive up with her. . . .

"County clerk's office," answered a female voice.

"This is Claire-Therese Rossiter, and I'm calling from the city," she said, trying to compose her unsteady voice. "I have the most absurd problem. When I was in Fulton Falls today for a hearing, I accidentally picked up the wrong briefcase. It was a foolish mistake, and I'm so embarrassed. Anyway, I have in my possession the papers of a man named Van Vierssen."

"Oh, yes, Nick Van Vierssen from the prison."

"That's the man, yes. Is there any way you could locate Mr. Van Vierssen and have him call me back? He must be greatly distressed by this."

"I can try."

"Oh, please do. Have him call my cell phone," she said, giving the woman her number. "If he's gone for the day, would you be kind enough to phone the prison and leave a message for him? I'll be at the Embassy Hotel after seven this evening, but he can still reach me by cell phone."

"All right. The Embassy Hotel after seven. I'll see that he gets your message."

"Thank you so much."

The woman clicked off. Claire plopped down in an over-stuffed chair backstage. If she started practicing again, she might not hear the phone. And if Nick Van Vierssen was still in the courthouse, he would call as soon as he got the message. She'd already caused the man a great deal of frustration; he didn't need extra rings of a phone. She had difficulty deciding just what she would say to him when he finally did call. She had no way of knowing how he'd react.

Because he dealt with legal matters, it wouldn't surprise her if he were less than civil over the phone, despite his easygoing manner in the courthouse snack bar.

As the minutes moved along, however, her dread became pleasant anticipation. It would be sort of a thrill to have him talk to her—even if he were angry.

When the phone rang, she bolted up and quickly answered it.

"Mr. Van Vierssen?" she asked.

"Yes. Is this Ms. Rossiter?"

She had difficulty controlling her quavering lips to say "Yes."

"I hear you have a briefcase that belongs to me."

His voice sounded just as free from anxiety as it had during the discussion with the men at the courthouse. For this she was supremely thankful.

"I do have it," she stumbled along, insecure, as she pictured the impressive face that went with the Nick-voice. "Please forgive me. I must have grabbed it by mistake in the snack bar."

"That's what happened, I'm sure."

"What inconvenience I've caused you. How did you ever get through your meetings?"

"Oh, I recited the Gettysburg Address a few times and then leaped boldly into Henry the Fifth's Agincourt appeal to his troops. I managed to hold my own in one session with my oratory."

Because she had studied him so thoroughly in the snack bar, she could imagine him thrusting his lower lip up over the upper after making such a droll comment, his eyes alert for the expected playful response.

Chuckling, she offered, "Seriously, it had to have been awkward. I hope I wasn't responsible for some poor prisoner missing out on his parole."

He laughed heartily with a strong baritone resonance. "No, nothing quite that world-shattering."

She recalled the way his lips separated when he laughed, erasing any tension others might have with him. By that laugh she knew he wasn't too out of sorts with her.

"I only had one meeting this afternoon," he added. "I could have used some of my notes, but they weren't absolutely necessary. If the papers had been confidential, I wouldn't have left the briefcase unlocked and on that shelf. So you see, you worried needlessly. However, tomorrow, it would help if I had the pamphlets."

"Of course. I'm going to drive to Fulton Falls as soon as we hang up. I realize the courthouse will be closed, but just tell me where I can meet you, and I'll be there."

"You won't have to do that. I'm going to be in the city tomorrow. My meeting's at eleven. I could pick up my papers before that meeting."

"Are you sure? I really don't mind driving up tonight."

"No, no. I'm serious. It's no problem. You're staying at the Embassy Hotel, right?"

"Yes, but I plan to be here at Lincoln Center's Tully Hall at nine and remain here throughout the day."

"You're going to be at the auditorium *all day* tomorrow?"

"Yes, I'll be practicing. I have a recital tomorrow night."

"Really! You're a soloist of some sort?"

"I'm a pianist."

"Outstanding," he replied enthusiastically. "All right, then. I'll stop by at the auditorium around nine-thirty. . .with *your* briefcase in tow. It was the only one left in the snack bar, so I figured someone had taken mine by mistake. Like you, I took the liberty of opening it to determine its owner."

"Oh? Of course," she mumbled, trying to picture the attractive warden going through the music in her briefcase. Had she left anything there that might prove embarrassing to her? No, not that she could recall.

"Fortunately, I didn't have to look far," he continued. "There was a letter on top with an address to a Ms. Rossiter at the university, plus a subpoena with your name on it."

As he continued, he made no mention of the interchange he had had with her when she and the waitress had exited the snack bar. He apparently didn't connect her voice with that incident.

"I phoned the university and left word with them," he explained. "So I was expecting your call—but not from the city. It works out much better for me this way."

"I'm relieved about that."

"You'll have your music or whatever you need in the morning. No later than ten o'clock."

"Actually, I have everything down for the recital. There's no rush."

"If you don't mind my asking, what are you performing?"

"Bach, Haydn, a jazz variation, some Liszt. Do you like Liszt?"

"Yes, he's one of my favorites. Are you playing any Rachmaninoff?"

"Not this time."

"Too bad. If I were a pianist I'd always play something by Rachmaninoff."

"I bet you'd be sensational," she commented, recalling his height, which would suggest he'd have hands with great power and reach. "You'd give me a lot of competition."

"Er, no, I don't think so," he said in a hesitant way that rather puzzled her, but only in passing.

"You just have your hands full taking care of prisoners," she said with a coy impudence.

"That's about it, yes. So, until tomorrow then, don't practice too hard, Ms. Rossiter—Ms. Claire-Therese Rossiter, is that right?"

"Yes, that's what it says on subpoenas and programs, because I'm Swiss-French, from Montreux. Some folks still address me by the whole hyphenated mouthful, but I've been known to answer to Claire all by itself just as readily."

"Well, then, Claire, don't wear yourself out practicing. Save some steam for the recital."

"I'll try to."

After he clicked off, she attempted to return to the piano and the Haydn that needed extra work because of the sluggish G, but her mind wouldn't focus on the job at hand.

Nicklaus Van Vierssen played havoc with her thoughts. The low resonance of his voice seemed far more melodious and tantalizing than the theme from Haydn.

He hadn't been angry at all. Not pompous, condescending, or even annoyed. Just pleasantly congenial, if unpredictable, with a comfortable, security-blanket kind of ease, allowing her to relax in his presence.

Perhaps his children didn't walklock step to their bedrooms, after all.

Perhaps he had no children.

Oh, no, he'd have to have children. That whimsical hair almost cried out to be rumpled by a youngster. Those Arctic eyes—perceptive, yes, but so tenderly welcoming—those superbly crafted facial features—all needed to be passed on to another generation of Dutchmen. He would most definitely have to have children.

But maybe he didn't. Maybe he didn't even have a wife.

That was definitely wishful thinking; of course he had a wife. How long would a striking Siegfried like that go without a wife? Undoubtedly he'd be married to an exotic blond mannequin.

Claire tried to dismiss him from her mind. After all, the episode was over—or would be the next morning. Nicklaus Van Vierssen would bow out of her life and return to his prison world.

❧

Dinner with Henri Poncelet didn't have to be canceled after all. Claire was glad. She always looked forward to being with Henri.

He was almost the caricature of a Frenchman. Claire delighted in his overly dramatic Continental mannerisms—effusive compliments, gallant kissing of hands, flamboyant dressing.

Her delight, however, did not extend to his cavalier attitude about marriage—getting married one day, divorced virtually the next. Nevertheless, following her father's tolerant acceptance of Henri's shortcomings, she valued his friendship as a business adviser.

A partner with her father in an importing business for nearly twenty years, Henri was almost a family member, the only "uncle" she would ever know.

Four months of the year he and his daughter Yolande lived

in Paris, the remainder of the time in the States. Whenever they found themselves in the same city, Claire and Henri would meet for dinner. He made Herculean efforts to attend her recitals.

❧

Claire opened the door of her hotel room to receive Henri, and he swooped in, kissing not only her hand but both cheeks as well. "Claire-Therese, how is it possible for an already magnificent woman to grow more enticing by the day? *Mais oui*, it is true. Your hair looks regal in a chignon."

Henri had grown a goatee that made him look more the *bon vivant* than on his previous visit. She suspected he'd also dyed his hair, because she didn't see a strand of his former premature gray lurking anywhere.

"So, are you ready for tomorrow?" he asked. "You've planned an ambitious program."

"I know. The Liszt is strenuous, and I'm a bit edgy about the Haydn. All in all, I think the selections will go well."

"Wasn't that Bach selection one of your father's favorites?"

"It was." Tears still beaded in her eyes when she thought of her darling papa. He'd been so devoted to her, spending a fortune for the best piano coaches in Paris and New York. After her mother's death, he'd never remarried. Claire became the center of his world.

"So, how was the trip down from the university?" he asked, adjusting his jacket collar. "Wasn't this the day you were to report for that hearing? What are you snickering about?"

"Something amusing occurred."

"I can't imagine anything amusing about a collision hearing."

"I made a careless mistake, Henri," she replied, proceeding to relate the details of the briefcase episode.

"What a dilemma for the wretched fellow," he responded in a tone that asked for further details.

"He was extremely civil."

"I would have been furious. Without a briefcase or my laptop, I'm helpless."

"You would have thrown a Napoleonic fit. Well, anyway, this man didn't. Actually, I half expected him to because he has a high-pressure job. He's a prison warden."

"A what?" asked Henri, his eyes wide with curiosity.

"A warden—or something like that—at a place called Everettsville."

"You're not serious?"

"I am. He's an intriguing guy." She ran her palm slowly across the right side of her swept-back hair. "On the surface he's the embodiment of carefree *GQ*. But beneath this exterior, through his conversation with associates he conveyed intense dedication to his work. His demeanor didn't match his job."

Henri studied her for a few moments, his voice becoming grave. "Everettsville's a massive, forbidding place. You've never heard of it?"

"No, never."

"It's on Route 54, beyond the reservoir, just off the thruway. Maximum security. They had a riot there ten years ago. A guard and five or six prisoners were killed."

She shook her head in denial. Although she knew Everettsville would be an unpleasant place to work, she'd hardly thought of it as hazardous to the point of massacre. "How cheerful. Now let's talk about the rack and guillotine for a few more jollies."

"All I'm saying is that it's a grim place for anyone to work. The man you're meeting tomorrow must be a gutsy individual."

A shiver raced down her spine, anxiety taking over as she weighed the circumstances surrounding the charming young warden.

In an effort to restore a more upbeat tone for the evening, she quipped, "So I'm relieved we're not going to Everettsville for dinner tonight. The bread and water up there isn't served nearly as elegantly as ours will be tonight at the Chalet Royal."

Henri chuckled and patted her hand affectionately. "Indeed not, *chérie*. I have reservations for nine o'clock. And they're preparing your favorite—*Ris de Veau*."

three

The next morning, as Claire ran through her scales, she knew the tuner had done his job well—the piano responded perfectly.

It wasn't until she got to the fermata near the end of the Bach that she realized someone else was in the auditorium. She stopped abruptly.

Peering out across the dark seats, she called, "Mr. Van Vierssen—is that you?"

"Yes, good morning," a louder version of the snack bar voice replied from the blackened theater. "Please, don't stop. Johann Sebastian would have a fit. It's savagery to chop that fugue off and let it hang there incomplete. Go on; finish it."

Smiling with pleasure and impressed by his recognition of the composer, she dashed off the remainder of the piece with a lighthearted flourish.

"Marvelous," he called, as he came down the aisle. "Encore," he said from just below the stage.

She laughed. "Oh, how I wish Cahill of the *Times* were as easy to please as you."

She hurried over to the edge of the stage. Bending down on one knee, she squinted into the concert hall. She could see him now, standing in the aisle, ramrod stiff, his hands in the pockets of sand-colored trousers, topped by an olive jacket and an open-collared green and yellow plaid shirt. A stunning outfit—an arresting complement to his blond hair.

She was glad she'd worn slacks. It was easy to sit down on the edge of the stage.

"Your briefcase is there in the first row," she said, nearly tongue-tied; she was nervous about carrying on a one-on-one conversation with the Nick of the snack bar.

26

"I saw it, so I put yours there, too." He moved closer and spoke from only a few feet below her.

"I'm sorry about what happened," she said. "I'd like to think there's some way I could repay you for this inconvenience."

He grinned widely, his head cocked to one side, but he remained very straight, his hands still in his pockets.

"There's no need to be too hard on yourself, but if you do feel a twinge of guilt, you could erase most of it by letting me stay for a while to listen to you practice."

"I'm flattered."

"You deserve to be. I had no idea when I talked to you on the phone that you were so accomplished and well-known. After I hung up, I dug out the theater section of the *Times,* where I found quite a blurb on Claire-Therese Rossiter. This is no small event tonight. And the passage you just raced through proves without a doubt that you're worthy of the glowing *Times* critique."

"This has been a good year. I've been lucky."

"Luck doesn't produce that level of Bach. I'd say you most certainly have a God-given talent, but there have been thirty hours a day of practice, too, I'll bet."

"Some days it *seems* like thirty hours."

The article said you're a professor at State."

"An assistant professor."

"When you spoke to me in the courthouse snack bar, I would have sworn you were no older than a college *student.*"

"You remember me," she responded with delight.

"When I walked in here, I recognized you immediately. You and another woman had to body-wrestle me and my friends to exit, if I recall correctly."

Claire decided a few words of explanation were necessary. "She was a fellow witness on an accident case."

"I figured as much. She hardly came across as your mom. Courtrooms have a way of bringing all sorts of folks together."

Like you and me, she was tempted to say.

"Anyway," he went on, "I said to myself, that beautiful

young woman I'm about to talk with can't possibly be the pianist written up in the *Times*."

"If you were up here on the stage, you'd see beauty in short supply—gigantic calluses on my fingers; short, ugly, unpolished nails; wrinkles around my eyes from lack of sleep. . ."

"I saw no wrinkles in the snack bar, and that was at close range."

"That snack bar had a way of crowding out even the wrinkles," she said, laughing.

He laughed, too. A warm laugh. How easy he was to talk to. She felt as comfortable with him as she assumed his associates from the courthouse had been.

"I trust you've made some CDs," he said as his laughter subsided.

"I'm going to have a studio session on this tour. The CD will be released in October."

"Please write and tell me the release date, so I can buy one."

"Don't be silly. I wouldn't let you *buy* one. I'll send you one. Let me get my notepad." She scurried back to the piano for her pad and pencil so she could write down his address.

"It isn't necessary to feel obligated to me at all," he called over to her. "I'll be happy to go to a music store and—"

"Nonsense. I wouldn't hear of it." She scampered back to the edge of the stage and poised herself with a pad and pencil. "Where shall I send the CD?"

"You don't need to write anything down. Just mail it to Everettsville Prison with the same zip code as your subpoena. My title is deputy superintendent, security, but with or without my august title, I'll get it."

"You want me to send it to the prison?" she asked in a startled voice. "Not to a home address?"

"I live at the prison."

Her eyes widened in surprise. "You *live* there?"

"Yes, I have quarters on the grounds."

"Oh—well, er, I see. Okay, I'll send it out to you there. Fine.

And if you care to attend tonight's concert—I mean, if you'd really like to come, I can leave a ticket at the box office."

"That would be great. I'd love to come. However, early in the evening, I'm tied up; I couldn't get here much before nine." He lowered his head in thought. "But perhaps I could catch your finale or an encore." He smiled back up at her. "I'd like to come to at least part of the program."

"Marvelous. Why don't I leave several tickets and you can bring your wife, or. . ."

"One ticket will be adequate. Ah. . ." He paused, his discerning eyes suggesting he saw through her. "I don't have a wife. And I'll be so rushed getting here, it'll be best I come alone without friend or, er, coworker. So one ticket will be fine. Thank you."

He wasn't married. She was inordinately pleased by this revelation—more pleased, she knew, than she had a right to be. Common sense told her this terrific human being wasn't waiting around for her to bring arpeggios into his life.

"I'm glad you're coming," she continued. "I better be asked for an encore."

"You will be," he said decisively. "Anyway, I've kept you from your practicing much too long. Why don't I just sit here for a short while and let you continue."

"Actually, I *had* better put my fingers through their paces."

"Right." His voice took on an authoritative, Beethoven severity. "Back to vork, *Fräulein.*"

She giggled as she rendered him a theatrical cringe.

Her mood hardly seemed serious enough for practice. But discipline won out. Once she stretched her fingers a few times, she was ready to tackle Liszt.

The music had an exciting new pizzazz. Startled, she realized that having Nick Van Vierssen in the audience was not only relaxing, but thrilling. To a degree, it was as it used to be when her father had listened to her. Nick's presence brought her to new heights of performance.

As she neared the Liszt finale, she recalled that she hadn't

invited Nick to the reception planned for her at the Fontainebleau Club after the performance.

She played the final chord and glanced out at the seats.
Radiant, she waited for a comment or applause.

But there was neither. She walked over to the edge of the
stage. Nick had gone.

She wondered why his sudden absence gave her such a
sense of emptiness.

≈

The audience that evening proved to be remarkably large—
especially for a new artist. Claire was pleased with the enthusiastic response she received after the first half of her program.

During intermission, she made a special point to check her
hair and makeup, a good bit more makeup than she usually
wore. Emma, the waitress, would have applauded her effort.
Because Nick would be there for the final numbers, she
wanted him to be captivated, not only by her music, but also
by her appearance.

How immature I'm being, she tried to tell herself. Men had
come and gone in her life—dozens. Charming professors, such
as Dr. Ernst Griesing, whom she'd worshiped in Salzburg. And
fellow faculty members—Gerry Hawlin and Bill Lansing.

But never had she met a man like Nick, who devoted himself
to something so startlingly dangerous and out of the spotlight
as handling prisoners. What had prompted this sophisticated
young man to closet himself in a penitentiary far away from
the mainstream of civilization?

As she went out onto the stage for the second half of her
program, she wasn't thinking about critics in the audience.
She knew she'd be playing only for Nick.

Yet maybe that was why the Liszt went so well. Even by
her own standards, it was a sensation. The audience went wild
with applause.

Her jazz variations on a spiritual were successful also. But it
was the Liszt with its sudden fortissimo explosions that took the
house down. The audience called her back for three encores.

Well-wishers jammed the dressing room. Henri held her hand fawningly. Others embraced her. There were flowers everywhere. And *people* everywhere. Noise, confusion, festive chaos.

Even so, her eyes moved in wayward fashion, scanning the crowd for Nick.

As she hugged Elaine Adinolfi and later Bernadine Krueger, she peered over their shoulders to see if Nick had arrived.

Finally he *was* there—standing by the door, pillar-tall in a dark, conservative, well-tailored pin-striped suit that blended astonishingly well with his still undisciplined hair and loose tie. Some men had the capacity to carry off any combination of clothing and hair—Nick certainly was one of them.

In black suede gloves he held an enormous bouquet, a veritable garden of plum-colored roses.

"Excuse me, Bernadine," she sputtered, "there's a person I must greet. Pardon me a moment. . . ."

Weaving through the crowd, she noticed out of the corner of her eye that Henri was watching her intently.

"Nick," she called. It surprised her that she could call out his first name so readily after knowing him only one day. His smile indicated he was pleased she had.

"Claire, it was staggering," he responded with an exuberance that seemed mixed with an embarrassed shyness she hadn't expected.

"When did you arrive?" she asked.

"During the last movement of Haydn. Superlative. Then the Liszt—unreal. Were some of those stretches tenths?"

"Yes."

"I would have been bowled over by your performance tonight even if I'd never met you." He paused, his mouth twisting with an obvious lack of confidence, as if he were searching for the right words.

When he did speak, it was as if he had spent years in preparation for that speech, his lips barely enunciating the soft-spoken words. "The fact that I had met you, that I knew what a delightful person you are—well, that made the experience an event of major importance for me. But it wasn't only the music that was worthy of raves, Claire-Therese Rossiter. Your gown is elegant. *You* are supremely elegant, and then some."

He handed her the roses. "Careful now, don't let the thorns damage those splendid fingers."

"Thank you so much, Nick," she murmured, tearing her eyes away from his to look at the roses. "They're gorgeous. The edges are almost translucent—like amethysts. They must have been frightfully expensive."

"Mmmm, yes, somewhat. But how often do I have the opportunity to purchase flowers for a famous pianist? Women like you don't meander into a man's life every day of the week."

"Nick, I don't deserve any kind of gift after the anxiety I put you through about the briefcase."

"Hey, wait a minute. I'm glad you swiped the briefcase. It was a fortunate misadventure."

She brought the roses up to her face and all but kissed them. Then she remembered the reception. "Oh, Nick, we're all going to a party at the Fontainebleau Club in a few minutes. You'll join us, of course. . . ."

"I'm sorry, Claire. I'd like to but. . ."

How could he possibly turn down her invitation? He had no plans for the evening, or he wouldn't have attended the concert. Did he think he'd be a fish out of water?

Nonsense. He'd be a desirable asset to any gathering, no matter how mundane or upscale. Everyone would adore him. Even the discriminating Bernadine Krueger.

Henri would relish a few words with him about Everettsville.

"Oh, you *must* come with us," she insisted with a vehemence that surprised her. "Most of my friends have never encountered a man who does something as outlandish as you do for a living."

He laughed, but his laugh now had a hollow ring that made her uneasy. "I'm really sorry. Some other time." He stepped back out into the hallway. "I have to drive back to Everetts-ville tonight."

Staring at him in disbelief, Claire persisted, displaying uncustomary urgency. "An hour or two can't make a differ-ence, Nick. Certainly you're not declining because we've just met one another and you don't know my friends. You'll be very welcome—you know that, don't you?"

"Actually, I *do* know that, Claire."

"You wouldn't be an outsider; I wouldn't let you be."

"I'm sure you wouldn't. In fact, I can't imagine any situation where you wouldn't try very hard to make me comfortable."

"Then, why not come? The Fontainebleau Club is north of here, almost on your way. Come along with us for an hour or so. Have something to eat before your drive back."

"Claire, I can't swing it tonight," he said unconvincingly, as he became engulfed by the hallway crowd.

She attempted to follow. "I'll see you again, won't I, Nick?"

"I'm sure," he said, his arm up, his gloved hand offering a little wave. "I'll be looking for your CD in the mail. Bye now, Claire."

To her chagrin, Elaine Adinolfi got between them, making it impossible for Claire to return his wave.

"The aspic will be melty if we don't get up to the Fontaine-bleau soon," said Elaine. "It's a gloppy mess whenever we're late—oh, my, aren't those the loveliest roses."

"Yes, aren't they," replied Claire, studying them with a twinge of sadness.

"Rare indeed," added Henri, approaching them both. "And who might that gentleman have been, Claire? I've never seen him before."

"He's–he's the prison warden."

"You don't mean it," said Henri with a questioning turn of his mouth. "Interesting."

"A prison warden?" asked Elaine. "What's a prison warden doing here?"

"Oh, he's an old friend of Claire's," said Henri with a wink. "Her Chopin's hot stuff in the 'big house.' "

Claire tried to dismiss the subject with a polite chuckle.

But it wasn't quite so easy to dismiss Nick from her mind. He had made a great effort to get to her performance. His glance had all but screamed out his desire to be with her.

She was sure something unpleasant prevented him from accepting her invitation to the reception—an event that turned out to be the last word in elegance.

Hordes of prominent people attended. All were pleased that the evening had been a financial, as well as an artistic, success. She glowed as she mingled with her many friends and wealthy sponsors.

From the roof garden, the city lights spread to the horizon. This was a day she had looked forward to for so long.

It would have been ideal if Nick had come. Why did his absence cause her such unhappiness? Wasn't it foolish to dwell on him at all, someone she'd known for only a couple of hours?

Nevertheless, despite being in the company of the city's most aristocratic people, she missed him. He was the most fascinating man she'd ever met.

Later, as she went to bed, the last things she gazed at were the plum-colored roses in the vase by the dresser. She refused to believe Nick hadn't been attracted to her—that he wasn't thinking of her, as well—even though he'd chosen not to attend the reception in her honor.

four

With the exception of Philadelphia, the recitals in September went well. In Cincinnati, she experienced a singular event: perfection. She took bows to thunderous applause with a standing ovation from the jubilant crowd in the municipal recital hall.

How she wished Nick had been in Cincinnati.

To her dismay, however, she experienced emotional letdown in the days that followed Cincinnati. How could she ever put on a performance like that again? Claire was confronted by the worst kind of competition possible—herself! Herself, under ideal conditions.

In her final two programs, she played well—the audience was more than pleased. But when she returned to the university campus October 11, she felt exhausted in spirit as well as in body.

The following weekend, she didn't go to the piano at all. Instead, she sat for hours in her living room, studying the antics of her cat, a stray ragamuffin that she'd christened Galuppi after an insignificant Baroque composer, Baldassare Galuppi.

A student had cared for Galuppi during her concert tour, but the little creature had missed Claire. He was underfoot or sitting by her side constantly. One Sunday afternoon she found herself with Galuppi on her blue modular sofa, just staring at the grand piano.

As Claire scrutinized the room, she became aware of how spartan her home was. It looked more like a music store than a home—her impressive Steinway grand dominated the center of the living room, with electronic keyboards and a spinet against the walls on either side of the fireplace. "Nick would be horrified that a female could live in such a cell," she sputtered to Galuppi. "This place looks *worse* than a prison. Even the prisoner Zimblatz probably has pictures or something on the walls."

She had nothing.

Nick wouldn't be impressed with the place, she decided. But why should she care what Nick might think? She would never see him again. He'd made that obvious when he refused her invitation to the reception at the Fontainebleau Club.

Why should Nick Van Vierssen need her or her Fontainebleau Club? As if there weren't mobs of other events and people in his life, including, more than likely, an attractive, churchgoing girlfriend who was more "Christian" than Claire had the right to call herself.

What made her think a Nick-type guy would attach much significance to his buying roses and expressing appreciation for her music?

But she'd had enough experience with men to know they didn't buy exceptional bouquets like his merely as a backstage compliment. Nick Van Vierssen had thought through that purchase carefully, wanting *his* backstage flowers to be uniquely lovely.

So, she convinced herself, it *was* in the realm of possibility he might come to State sometime and look her up. If he did, he would see her miserable hovel.

The next day, she went into town and bought some things to brighten up her abode—two framed Picasso prints, a rather intricate macramé wall hanging, a hand-carved chess set with stand, and two handsome Peruvian pillows.

On her way home, she passed a flower shop, in the window of which she spied an outlandish plant with gigantic plum-colored flowers—not nearly so exquisite as the roses Nick had given her, but almost the exact same shade. He would think the plant gauche.

It *was* gauche. But it would look amusing and cheerful in her bay window. She absolutely had to have it.

And it *did* cheer the room up enormously. Galuppi liked playing games with its enormous leaves.

ᔐ

On Friday Claire received a phone call from the recording company, saying her tapes and CDs were available. They were to be distributed through the company's sales outlets immediately.

"As we told you," said the shipping clerk, "we're sending twenty to those friends of yours on the list you provided. Do you have any deletions or additions to that list?"

"No, I don't think so."

"The packaging's terrific, with a folded poster of you, Ms. Rossiter. A dandy shot. You don't find many classical pianists who are so good-looking. *I'm* even going to give a listen to your CD, and I don't usually dig that kind of music."

She chuckled at the candor of the clerk.

In a matter of days, Nick would be getting his CD. Maybe he'd phone to tell her he'd received it. She hoped he would. What a delight it would be to hear his voice again.

She had no trouble convincing herself it would be appropriate to write him to tell him to expect the CD. He wouldn't find such a letter out of order—a nice, friendly, casual letter.

She decided writing it personally on attractive stationery would be better than punching it out on a computer. But once she took pen in hand, she found she had difficulty putting appropriate thoughts on paper. Stating her true feelings was out of the question. To do less was maddening.

She tore up several attempts before she finally wrote a note that set the proper tone:

> *Dear Nick,*
>   *The recording company informed me that my CD is being released. They're sending one to you. Despite the fact that Rachmaninoff wasn't on my original program, I managed to polish up a brief prelude and squeeze it in—yes, just for you.*

My tour was satisfying, if exhausting, and I'm back at the university, teaching.

I hope I don't have to commit a heinous crime to see you again. If you're in the vicinity of State, drop by. I'll treat you to cheese fondue—the only thing, sorry to say, that I cook with finesse.

The roses lasted well over a week. Luckily, I was able to purchase an enormous Papa-Bear plant with blossoms of the same plum shade. I didn't want to exist in an amethyst-free environment after having the roses with me so long.

So, if you ever happen to be looking for my house on Regent Street, keep your eyes peeled for a plum-colored jungle in a bay window—that will be "me."

Most sincerely,
Claire

Nick's reply came a week later. It was in a plain, unadorned envelope with no special markings. Like the envelope, the letter was printed on a computer.

Dear Claire,

How sensational to receive your CD and charming letter. I've played the selections continuously. You're as good as Andre Watts!

I was thrilled with the Rachmaninoff that you included to please me. It's marvelous, the conclusion exceptionally brilliant. I'm in awe of your skill and accomplishment.

The promo shot of you that came with the CD couldn't be better. It vividly illustrates how magnificent you looked the night I met you backstage after your concert, many weeks ago now. An exciting event for both of us.

I wish you continued success in your endeavors. Be sure to set aside some time for your own compositions; you should be chugging away at more of those jazz variations.

Warmest regards,
Nicklaus Van Vierssen

And that was all. No suggestion they see one another again. No request that she write back. And even the hastily scrawled scratch-marks he passed off as a signature were his full, formal name, not just "Nick."

Why? The mood of the letter was completely informal. So upbeat. It didn't match the signature at all.

She considered phoning him. They could chat, and she could feel him out.

But she didn't have the courage to call. Her pride, her honest appreciation of her own worth, wouldn't allow her to beg attention from a man.

That evening she spent two hours playing Rachmaninoff, Galuppi resting under the grand and enjoying the vibrations while purring with satisfaction. She glanced over at the plum-colored plant.

"What did I say or do that turned him off?" she asked herself, recalling his obvious pleasure when he gave her the roses backstage.

But confounding her was the way he had melted into the crowd after refusing her invitation to the Fontainebleau Club—with a look on his face that seemed to say, "I want to go with you, but. . ."

Like a seacoast mist, the crowd had enveloped him, shrouding his reason for keeping his distance.

૨૦

It was Tuesday, and an astonished Claire had just read in the faculty newsletter—in an obscure article—that there was to be a seminar on prison reform in mid-November. It would be sponsored by the sociology department. Among the four guest speakers would be Nicklaus Van Vierssen, "the chief of security at Everettsville Prison."

She couldn't believe her eyes. Nick was scheduled to be on campus in a matter of weeks. He hadn't even mentioned this fact in his letter.

"He's going to surprise me," she mumbled halfheartedly. But the newsletter shook in her hand. Anger, frustration, or some indefinable emotion was taking hold of her.

"He doesn't have to make any big project out of this," she stormed aloud. "No major commitments whatsoever. He can be engaged, going into a monastery, or simply dead-set against marriage. But does that mean he can't call me to say hello? And tell me he's coming to this campus so I can make changes in my schedule to take in his presentation? Why wouldn't he want me there? What possible reason is there for this unexplainable behavior?"

Of one thing she was confident: He had no Freudian quirks. There were no psychotic aberrations, or he'd never have been hired to fill the job at Everettsville.

His demeanor was assertive, forthright, and masculine. When he looked into her eyes that night of the recital there had been desire for her. He had responded to her signals.

Then why? Why wouldn't he tell her he was coming to State?

Claire knew she could never keep herself away from that seminar. Curiosity, if nothing else, would force her to be present. She *had* to see Nick again, listen to his presentation, and find an opportunity to learn why he had behaved so strangely.

Her schedule showed a minor conflict on the Saturday morning of the seminar. Irene Dabrovsky was having a recording session for a Beethoven competition. The studio had already been reserved.

Irene had worked much too hard to be without Claire's guidance and assistance. There was no way to get out of that commitment.

But, Claire figured, the recording session would be over by eleven, which would give her time to hear part of the summations and see Nick during the lunch break.

According to the newsletter, the afternoon had been set up by the sociology department for student conferences with the guest lecturers. However, there would be a second open session at seven in the evening.

A wind ensemble concert was on her calendar for that

evening. All music department personnel were expected to attend. But it wasn't obligatory. She could miss the concert without too much censure from her department chairman.

The Monday before the seminar, she phoned the sociology department to get more details.

"Jim Gleason here," said the exuberant voice of the young chairman of sociology.

"Hello, Jim, this is Claire Rossiter."

"Claire! No fooling? What a surprise. To what do I owe this charming interruption to an otherwise tedious day?"

"I noticed you're having a seminar Saturday—on prisons. Well. . .er, I wanted to get more information because, quite frankly, I'd like to attend."

"Is this for real? I think you must have the wrong idea. We're not going to be discussing your kind of keys. No B-flat or F-sharp minor or anything like that. Just large, unwieldy things that clank and unlock clammy dungeons and snake pits."

She smiled, imagining Jim's merry eyes as he said these words. He was a great guy, an asset to any gathering. With Peg, his wife, he was a conspicuous sight on campus, the couple forever followed by dozens of children—not just their own, surely, but whole neighborhood's. The Gleasons, who attended her church, could be counted on to provide games and guitar-accompanied skits for Sunday school outings.

Frequently she saw Jim tossing baseballs to kids on the lawn behind Old Main or driving into a fast-food parking lot in his SUV. Always he had a big wave for her.

"I'm serious," she replied. "I want to attend because—um, you see, I have a friend who's a warden of a prison."

"Where? At the Bastille?"

"No, sorry. Anyway, I was wondering if any of the men on your panel have written articles or books that I might look over."

"They all have. You don't think I'd bring any second-rate Charlies up here to talk to my troops, not to the campus where we have such a celebrated pianist as Claire-Therese Rossiter on the faculty of music."

She grinned. "You're impossible."

"Impossible, am I? In my book, you're celebrated, lady. Tell you what: I'll run off some articles that I think are of interest and send them over to you."

"That would be fine. Thanks so much."

"Claire, by the way, if you're coming, why don't you give us a little rendition on the eighty-eight of 'Jailhouse Rock' as a curtain-raiser?"

"What would you say if I said, 'Okay, I will?' "

He snickered. "Hey, I'll accept that offer. Peg and I are having an open house at our place after the evening session. You can play 'Jailhouse Rock' there for the edification of our guests. How's that?

"Seriously," he continued, "how 'bout coming to the party? A couple of those speakers are single. They wouldn't mind looking at the likes of you over the cheese dip. What do you say? Since you like prisons, you might enjoy the informal conversation. I'm sure it'll cover such scintillating topics as 'How I spread-eagled Pretty Boy Maloney'—that sort of thing. Shall I tell Peg you'll be there?"

She had to let Jim ramble on because she honestly didn't know how to reply to his invitation. Thoughts raced through her mind. Would Nick want her there? If she could only *know* if he wanted her there—or even wanted to see her at all—then she would be able to give Jim an answer.

"Claire, are you still with me?" asked Jim.

"Yes–yes, Jim, I'm still here. About Saturday night, I'm not sure. I can't say right now. There's a departmental concert that night. The wind ensemble—"

"The *what?*"

"The wind ensemble."

"Why, it's my patriotic duty to rescue you from an evening like that. You get yourself to my place. We'll be expecting you."

"Jim, I'm not sure."

"You be there—ya hear? I'll get those articles to you tomorrow morning."

❧

The next day Claire set aside her whole lunch hour to read the articles Jim had sent over.

She had to devour Nick's first. Taken from a national magazine, it was written for the general public in a concise and readable fashion.

To her chagrin, a biography had been torn away. This exasperated her because she yearned to know more about Nick—his early life, where he'd gone to college, why he'd chosen a career in corrections, how he'd experienced such a close bond with God. A biographical sketch might even have given her a clue as to why he behaved so unpredictably with her.

But there was a picture of him. She studied it for a long time. His eyes seemed to be accusing her, telling her it was wrong to possess him, even a picture of him. Yet the picture was precious to her. At least a representation of Nick could remain in her life.

In the article, he wrote: "As deputy superintendent in charge of security, I'm responsible for keeping order and preventing escapes, riots, and personal injury. My background in engineering as well as corrections allows me to keep abreast of state-of-the-art technology to ascertain the most efficient and economical ways to confine men securely. The expenditures for more attractive and more open facilities must be carefully weighed to evaluate the degree to which they will improve the rehabilitation and safety of prisoners, and, I might add, the safety of the corrections staff who must keep them incarcerated."

The article went on to describe revolutionary new prisons in Chicago and Los Angeles. Apparently, an equally new complex was being constructed at Everettsville.

"We mustn't expect miracles from ferroconcrete, plastic, and electronics," the article concluded. "New prisons will not eliminate the need for competent, dedicated corrections personnel.

But when cutting-edge technology can assist these officers to better care for the inmate population, then we heartily support it."

There was no attempt in the article to come off as a uniquely qualified specialist. Or a martyr. It was just a straightforward evaluation of the innovations of penitentiaries around the country, Everettsville in particular.

She looked again at his picture. For no good or sensible reason, she felt optimistic that her encounter with him on Saturday would not be unpleasant and would provide a few answers to the multitudes of questions she wanted to ask him.

In all of her instructions and practicing sessions Thursday and Friday, concentration was all but impossible. She spent both evenings on her blue modular sofa, petting Galuppi and thinking out a strategy for greeting Nick if he should phone.

But he didn't phone. Even on Friday night there was no phone call.

It infuriated her to know he must be somewhere in town— maybe at Jim's, right in town within walking distance—and he didn't phone.

She had dressed in a vibrant red, *"tres chic"* jumpsuit, in case he stopped by. But by ten o'clock she knew he had no intention of doing that. She put her head down on the sofa, tears forming in her eyes, her spirit in an emotional chasm between anger and disappointment.

five

Thankfully, on Saturday Irene Dabrovsky was so well prepared for the recording session that Claire was able to get
away by 10:30.

She grabbed her coat and all but ran to the Student Union.
The conference room was packed, every seat taken. A large
crowd stood near the entrance as well.

Someone was already speaking. It sounded like Nick, but the
amplification distorted the voice, so Claire couldn't be sure.

She craned her neck to see who it was. A man ahead of her
moved sufficiently to the left that she could view the dais.

Yes, it was Nick—standing behind the big old maple lectern.
The ceiling lights of the auditorium seemed to be panning his
hair for gold, highlighting shades of lemon only to move on to
bronze. He had made a trip to his barber-stylist, she noted,
because the strands on his forehead were both shorter and less
wayward than at the recital.

She was queasy at the sight of him, wanting to rush up
there to make her presence known.

It was a question/answer period. A gangly student had
arisen to challenge Nick on some point he'd made. "You're
not too optimistic about the new prisons," the student retorted
with condescension.

"Optimistic in what way?" Nick asked.

"Well, you seem to think prisoners won't be reformed no
matter what kind of place they're in."

"When it comes to the type of inmates I work with at
Everettsville, I'm not convinced a high-tech building will
work miracles in the rate of recidivism. That doesn't mean we
shouldn't avail ourselves of new materials and make a prison
as pleasant as possible."

Nick leaned over the lectern and looked at the student. "The laminated polycarbonate windows, for example, are an improvement over bars. As I mentioned earlier, electronic impulses penetrate these windows, telling us instantly of an impending escape. We have closed-circuit surveillance in all corridors. So we're able to minimize the number of guards needed in direct-contact situations. Anytime I can relieve an officer of duty in a contact situation, I'm overjoyed, but—"

The student interrupted. "Most prisoners have had a rough life. A decent environment might help them turn themselves around."

Nick didn't answer right away. Yet he didn't appear ill-at-ease. He seemed to have no nervous mannerisms—no tapping on the lectern, no rubbing of his chin. The only animated part of his body remained his expressive face—now deadly serious, with no trace of a smile.

"Keep in mind that Everettsville houses violent men. I agree; most come from unhealthy environments. But not necessarily a ghetto."

"What are you getting at?" the student pursued with a sarcastic edge to his voice.

Nick went on. "Many inmates at Everettsville cruised in the jet set before their convictions. If we replaced steel bars with cocktail bars or a gym with parallel bars, most of our best efforts would be a comedown for them."

He paused for a brief grin. "A lot have been fat cats. They've had custom sports cars and stayed in the best resorts. In some cases they *owned* the resorts. Physical plants, alone, won't work miracles."

A young woman a few rows to Claire's left leaped to her feet, her hand pummeling the air to be recognized.

Nick acknowledged her. "Yes, miss?"

"In old prisons human beings were caged animals. Most criminals may never have known love even if they owned posh resorts."

Nick's expression showed he liked the girl's spunk.

"We probably *don't* dispense enough loving-kindness. Basic sympathy often wears thin," he said, somewhat tongue in cheek, standing tall once again.

"Several years ago, we built an outside visiting area—new picnic tables, baseball diamond, playground equipment for children, the works. We open this area several times a week. But every time—without exception—we have contraband brought into the prison. Policing the area's not easy."

Claire listened with rapt attention, recalling the comments of Nick's friends in the courthouse snack bar. They had thought Nick tough. He was talking tough now.

"Nearly every prisoner at Everettsville strategizes to get contraband into the prison—crack, heroin, liquor—items that threaten security and can be used for services rendered within the walls. We find heroin in heels of women's shoes, crack carried in balloons in the mouth, liquor in resoldered orange juice cans. Many inmates control empires of crime on the outside, people ready to do their bidding. What would occur, I ask you, if someone got explosives into the compound?"

Explosives!

Claire's eyes scrunched up in disbelief. Everettsville could conceivably be a war zone. Why did Nick choose to *live* there?

"Also, don't forget," he went on, "we can be sued if inmates are abused, or become infected with AIDS."

A wide grin broke across Nick's face. "All's not lost, however, even at Everettsville. I'll have positive things to say in my presentation tonight. It's time for your next speaker, though, my friend Arnold Saxby. He's an expert on juvenile facilities, where a swimming pool and chocolate shakes *can* make a difference."

As he concluded, Nick received enthusiastic applause from the students, many of whom stood up directly in front of Claire. She couldn't see the dais at all.

When the applause died down, she heard someone introducing Arnold Saxby.

The students took their seats. Claire got a glimpse of the new speaker, also a young man, with an oversized beard and more laid-back clothing than Nick's. His talk began with light-hearted lampooning of Nick's reputed severity.

She couldn't see Nick, but she could hear his laughter. It was evident from Arnold Saxby's comments that he and Nick had been sparring partners before.

Claire found it almost impossible to concentrate on the Saxby presentation, though. All she could think of was Nick, sitting up there beyond view in the same room as her.

Twenty minutes later, when the session was over, the students mobbed the dais to speak to the participants. A photographer snapped pictures. There was the usual din of an assembly dispersing.

She spied Jim Gleason. He seemed to be studying her as he sauntered over, a questioning smirk on his mischievous round face.

"So, Claire, you have a friend who's a warden. That friend couldn't be one of my guest speakers, by any chance?"

Embarrassed, she sputtered, "Are you suggesting that—"

"That you showed particular interest in one of them? Yes. I was watching you as Nick Van Vierssen was speaking. You were on tiptoes the whole time."

She'd have to admit the obvious. "Okay, I'm acquainted with Nick. We met in Fulton Falls several months ago under wild circumstances. I walked off with his briefcase by accident."

"Did he plop you in solitary?"

"He was pretty decent about the whole thing. Anyway, it was the beginning of—well, a friendship of sorts. I had never met a corrections officer and considered Nick a rather remarkable person."

Jim's expression became more sober. "Nick's only a little short of awesome."

"Awesome, you say. That's a pretty heady evaluation."

"He's the big man in our lives, Peg's and mine. We're pleased to admit he's nearly one of the family."

"Really—does he come here often?"

"No, he has a difficult time breaking out of that loony bin he inhabits. We see him only a few times a year. Sometimes we ski together. He's a great skier—even does some jumping. But most of the time when we get together we can only fit in a few games of Ping-Pong."

She glanced toward the dais at Nick, who was still surrounded by the crowd. It was fun studying him from afar—learning new insights into his character. She imagined him wearing ski goggles, shushing down a slope at sixty miles an hour, then soaring through the air after taking off from a ski jump.

"Watching him play Ping-Pong is something else again," Jim went on. "He always draws a crowd. Surprisingly, crowds don't bother him."

She smiled and turned back to Jim, picking up the thread of the conversation.

"He draws a crowd, hmmm? For Ping-Pong? He doesn't look like the type who'd be playing Ping-Pong seriously. Skiing, yes; sailing, definitely. But Ping-Pong? No. So you're not in his league in the art of table tennis. Does Nick beat you all the time?"

Jim's eyes glinted accusingly, which disarmed her. "He doesn't beat me all the time. No," he said hesitatingly.

She was bewildered by Jim's obvious discomfort.

Finally, Jim finished his statement, "But Nick's some kind of fierce for a guy with no hands."

She laughed politely.

Jim actually glared at her, seething with what appeared to her to be a hard-to-control rage.

Flustered by his behavior, she stammered. "Forgive me, Jim; I'm not up on table tennis jargon." Why was he staring at her so menacingly? "A guy with no hands—I don't understand what that expression means," she continued, bewildered.

Jim's fury subsided. His eyelids appeared weighted by sadness. "Claire, I thought you said you knew Nick!" he said slowly. "When I said he had no hands, I meant just that—he has no hands. He's an amputee."

The blood rushed in a torrent from her head to her feet. She felt faint as she stared at Jim. He seemed to be fading. She groped for him and then grabbed his arm, trembling violently.

"No hands. That's not true. I've seen Nick numerous times—on three occasions. . . ."

"It *is* true, Claire. I can't imagine how you could have seen him on even one occasion and not known. He rarely—if ever—conceals the fact."

"Nooooo," she groaned, shaking her head in firm denial. She turned to the dais where Nick was smiling with the other men for pictures. "Not Nick. Not that man up there. I know it's not true. He gave me flowers after my concert—using his hands. At least one of them. He waved goodbye to me. I tell you, Jim, I *saw* his hands that night of my recital. He had on black gloves and. . ."

"Did you touch either of his hands, Claire? Did he touch you with one?" Jim asked, his demeanor now filled only with compassion.

She suppressed a scream with her fists. "Oh, God, oh, my dear God," she gulped out, making a genuine attempt at prayer, seeking strength from a long-neglected Lord. "You mean that hand that waved to me was. . . ?"

"An artificial hand—a prosthesis—probably operated by an electronic device. Nick has many different prostheses." Jim touched her shoulder. "Claire, I'm sorry I had to be the one to tell you. And in such a crude and unfeeling fashion."

"I've got to get out of here," she managed, through jaws that seemed to be locking. "I've—oh, Jim, please get me out of here. I can't let Nick see me. Help me out of here before I become ill and create a scene."

Putting his arm around her, Jim led her down the corridor to an unused office. Then he closed the door and assisted her into a chair.

"Let me get you some ice water, you poor kid."

She shook her head. Ice water wouldn't do the trick. "Just sit with me," she implored while she tried to let the reality sink in.

"For a few minutes, Claire, but I have to get back to those guys and escort them to lunch."

"To lunch?" she stammered. How under the sun could a man with no hands eat lunch? How could he play Ping-Pong? Or ski? Or handle all the myriad activities of life?

"Let me get this straight, Jim. Right now, Nick has artificial electronic fingers on both hands. They look like flesh and blood fingers, but. . ."

Jim pulled a chair from behind a desk and sat down next to her. "That's not exactly true, Claire. Today Nick has the ersatz hand on one arm, and on the other he's using metal Greifer pincers."

"Pincers?" Her eyes were wild. Nick was using metal pincers?

Jim gripped her hand tightly. "Claire, this is an awful blow to you, but I assure you Nick is not to be pitied. He's adjusted to this handicap. So has everyone who knows him. When our family thinks of Nick, we just associate the Greifers with him as you would a pair of eyeglasses with someone else."

"You don't honestly believe Nick thinks of those metal things the way you and I might think of a pair of glasses?"

"Actually, I do. What's more to the point, *you* must try to look at them that way."

"I could never do that!" She got up and went over to the window, leaned on the sill, and began to sob convulsively. She couldn't control the painful wrenching in her stomach.

"So," she moaned, "this is the awful secret. This is why Nick didn't tell me he was coming here. It had nothing to do with how he felt about me. He just didn't want me to know he was an, an. . ."

"Ordinarily he's very candid about his handicap, Claire. He's a man of enormous spiritual depth. In fact, he told me once he thinks his handicap has made it possible for him to have a ministry to prisoners. An encounter with some handicapped kid somewhere prompted him to pursue this mission he believes he has. He gives lots of talks in rehab centers—works with kids who've lost limbs. His handicap is not something he usually hides."

"I tell you, Jim, he tried to hide it from me. Perhaps because I'm a pianist."

"Possibly. He may have thought you'd be uncomfortable playing in front of him."

"And he would have been correct." She turned to face Jim. "I will never play for him again. Oh, Jim, you don't know how grossly I behaved. I sent him a CD of my music. I remember even asking him if he played the piano. What must he have thought?"

"I'm sure he enjoyed your CD. He's a connoisseur of classical music. All kinds of music, for that matter."

She tried to sort through the words she'd spoken to Nick during their moments together. How many inappropriate things had she said to him in her ignorance? So delightful was his manner and repartee, so pleasant were the words they'd exchanged, she had trouble recalling statements she'd made that might have been painful for him.

She decided to force her mind onto another track. "How did it happen, Jim? Was he born. . .?"

"He was a midshipman at Annapolis—a junior, I think."

"A midshipman; yes, he fits the part."

It was easy to picture him in his whites at the Naval Academy, a bright future lying ahead for him.

Jim continued. "He was on a training cruise. A defective weapon exploded; a petty officer and another midshipman were killed. There was a fire and—"

"Oh, no." She closed her eyes, the tears flowing, her head throbbing. How tragic. Such a young man. . .his life just beginning. "Those first few weeks and months must have been. . ."

"Horrendous. Yes."

She began to shake once again. Jim moved over to her and held her arms tightly.

"Did you know him then?" she stammered, as the shaking began to abate.

Jim released her slowly. "No, I met him in grad school. We had a sociology course together. Peg and I were going through a bad time, and I felt myself a martyr. Then I ran smack into this no-handed so-and-so who seemed to have things all straightened out for himself."

Jim walked away from her. He scratched the side of his face as he added, "I wanted to know what his secret was. When he told me it was simply because he'd become a Christian, I didn't believe him."

"It couldn't be that simple."

"He just said that he'd become convinced Jesus Christ planned his agenda with good things in mind. As the weeks became months and I studied this incredible guy—his fortitude, his optimism, his sense of humor and consideration for others, his indomitable faith in God—I knew I had to check into the Jesus angle further. Peg and I did, and hey, the Holy Spirit brought a million blessings into our lives. They've never stopped coming."

"I see." Her throat seemed constricted, her thoughts so clouded, she wasn't able to give her full attention to Jim. She was in no mood, anyway, for a Sunday school lesson.

She sat down on the corner of the desk. "How could God have any kind of purpose in crippling a great guy like Nick?" She sputtered, "That kind of thinking is beyond me."

"It's not up to us to understand everything, Claire, though Nick could provide a more satisfactory answer to your question than I can."

She inhaled deeply and stared up at the ceiling. "You've got to get back to your guests, Jim," she went on, shaking her head. "Nick and the others must have their lunch."

"I hate to leave you like this."

"I'll manage. Go on, Jim."

"I'm not sure you're all right alone."

She rubbed a knuckle back and forth across her forehead. A hysterical laugh came forth. "How does anyone become 'all right' again after learning something like this about a person who, who. . ."

She waved her palm in a signal for him to leave. "Just go now, Jim. Honestly, I'll pull myself together and get home okay."

Jim went to the door. "Claire, why don't I tell Nick you're here and that you know everything. He'd put your mind at ease with a few good jokes. . . ."

Her eyes all but jumped out of their sockets. "Don't you dare tell him I'm here. Don't tell him anything about what happened to me. I simply couldn't face him now. I'm not sure I can *ever* see him, with his metal pincers for. . ."

She went over to Jim and grabbed his arm. "Promise me you won't tell him."

"Claire, tonight—you'll come to my home to the open house?"

She'd forgotten about the open house. "There's no way, Jim," she said, shaking her head. "I'm sorry."

He stared at her several minutes, his eyes filled with both sympathy and regret. "Nick needs someone so much in his life, if only to date on occasion. He deserves a break, Claire. Please come this evening."

"Impossible. I've just been torn in two by this disclosure, and you're asking me to rally and go to a party."

"How will you feel tomorrow, Claire, if you don't speak to Nick all weekend and he leaves never knowing you're aware of his handicap? Even if there's no big romance between you two, apparently a friendship has evolved. Are you going to sabotage that friendship because the guy has prostheses instead of hands? How will you be able to?"

"Stop it! Stop it right now, Jim," she stormed. "The scenario goes this way, remember? He didn't tell me he was coming here. *He* didn't want to see *me*."

"Come now, Claire. You know better than that. You've nailed the reason he didn't want to see you. That reason doesn't exist anymore."

Jim was correct. She hated to admit it, but she would indeed despise herself in the weeks to come if she didn't speak to Nick.

"Forgive me," she apologized, closing her eyes to Jim's scrutiny. "I shouldn't be angry with you. You're right. I should take the initiative and do *something*. But frankly, I don't know how I can get through an evening with him. I respect and admire him so much—he's so self-assured and dynamic. I mustn't weep in his presence."

"Why don't you see how things look this evening? As a professional performer, you've been in many tense situations before and come out fine. So this is a performance of a different kind. Give it a try." He opened the door. "I'll see you later, I hope. Listen to that crowd, Claire. There's still a big group down there. And Nick's having such a great time with those kids."

She bit her lip and nodded.

"He'll put you at ease, Claire. He's had this handicap so long that he's a veteran at making people comfortable with it. Try to come tonight." He winked at her as he closed the door behind him.

But after Jim left, she wept herself into exhaustion. Only when she was sure not a soul remained in the hallway did she sneak out and leave by a back exit.

Once home, she cried out to the walls, "Darling Nick, what frustration I've caused you, pounding away at tenths in Liszt, adding to your discomfort."

Pictures emerged again in her mind—of Nick as a midshipman, trim in those whites. So physically perfect, with dozens of girlfriends, surely. Then to have such an accident—the gross mutilation, the helplessness, the months of rehab. She shuddered, thinking of the embarrassment of having to wear metal contraptions and having people stare. It was so unspeakably unfair, so grim.

There was a maternal impulse that urged her to run to him wherever he was and to hug him away from curious hordes.

Yet at the same time, deep down in the recesses of her mind was another little voice that told her to flee from any further encounter with him while there was still a chance.

Most considerately, he hadn't contacted her so she would not have to experience his disfigurement. She *must* have been in his thoughts when he arrived on campus.

If she didn't attend the party—if she left well enough alone—she probably would never see him again, a detestable outcome based solely on her cowardice.

She realized she had to force herself to go to Jim's open house. However, she'd have to convince Nick she'd known all along that he was an amputee; he must never learn about the scene of this afternoon.

But how could she fool a man who analyzed facial expressions with such skill?

She'd have to be more successful than Zimblatz had been. It would be the performance of her lifetime, and she'd deserve more than a Schumann Medal if she pulled it off.

six

As she dressed for the evening programs, Claire's thoughts centered on the complications Nick must have, doing even the most basic things. How could he knot a tie? Buckle a belt? Put on socks? How, with such an appalling handicap, did he manage those things?

And a million others.

She drew her hair up into the chignon and put on simple gold earrings. It was, she decided, imperative that she stuff her purse with tissue—in case she fell apart and had to rush to an adjacent room to weep, all over again. She tossed on her charcoal coat and, with hesitancy, pulled fur-lined gloves from her pockets. It was chilly, and she needed them.

Nick would never need gloves.

As at the earlier session, there was a large crowd in the auditorium. She sat on the left side of the hall—in the middle of a row, to be as inconspicuous as possible.

Arnold Saxby was the first onto the dais behind Jim Gleason. Nick held the door for the two older speakers with what would have to be the plastic hand prosthesis. As they went past, he apparently said something amusing, because they both began to laugh uproariously.

Then as the three approached, she saw it—attached to his right arm was the prosthesis with the mechanical pincers. What had Jim called it? A Griffin? No, a Greifer. With it, Nick was holding his familiar briefcase.

It obviously was a routine thing for him. He really was an amputee. And shock above all shocks, he *did* accept that fact. Yet to her, this was all too new to accept. It was like a masquerade, as if someone were attempting that old pirate trick— any moment he'd drop the pincers to the floor and the normal hand would come out of his sleeve. Ta da! He would then wave to the crowd, trick completed.

But no such magic was forthcoming.

The dais was arranged informally with five chairs around a conference table. Microphones had been set up for each speaker.

Nick sat on the end closest to her, but faced the right side of the hall.

In stupefied horror, she studied him. With the prostheses he opened the briefcase and painstakingly extracted his papers. For sure, he deserved more applause than she did performing Bach fugues. The hours of practice that must have gone into such an achievement staggered her mind. If she'd thought of him as remarkable in the Fulton Falls courthouse, her admiration had increased a hundredfold.

When finally he rested his arm on the table, the prostheses were hidden from view, and Claire was able to give her attention to the rest of his person. He wore a preppie Harris tweed jacket, his conventional loose-collared shirt, and a rust-colored tie. His trousers were a dark reddish-brown. With sadness she noted that his well-polished brown loafers had no laces to tie.

As before, his blond hair couldn't escape the ceiling lights of the auditorium.

Jim made the introduction, announcing the evening's topic: the future of prisons in the United States. As he opened the floor to the first man, Samuel Schwartz, his eyes picked her up in the audience. A smile came to his lips. She returned a halfhearted nod.

Samuel Schwartz and the second speaker discussed, with equal pessimism, the lack of success they'd had with innovative policies. By contrast, Arnold Saxby, who followed, lauded the efforts made at his detention center.

Nick was last. He glanced out over the audience for several moments before he spoke. Then he began with a startling statement: "Well, how does it feel to be in prison?"

The crowd snickered. A few students made disparaging

remarks about the university.

"All of you should know what it's like," Nick continued, "because you're all incarcerated, after all—in prisons of your own creation, or society's."

Some of the students leaned forward in their chairs.

"Mature people know that for a society to function smoothly, individuals must accept certain forms of enslavement, putting handcuffs and fetters on their behavior. Whenever we make a commitment to somebody or something—husband or wife, children, a job, an education, faith in God—we relinquish freedom to do and say whatever we'd like, whenever we'd like. Each one of you has had to do that most of your life, or you wouldn't be in this university or in this room. I wouldn't either."

He glanced toward Claire's side of the room, so she slunk down in her chair. His eyes missed her.

"We're childish," he continued, "to the degree that we're unable to manacle our hostilities and demands, or to the extent we deprive others of their rights and privileges.

"Once in a while, however, even the most mature adult acts in a childish manner. I do myself, often. Sometimes, with my handicap, I try the impossible, and it boomerangs."

He was actually *talking* about his handicap, Claire realized. How could he call attention to something so horrible?

He now rested both prostheses on the table, in plain sight of the audience. "Once, a few years ago," he began again, "when I first began wearing artificial hand machinery, I played soccer with some neighborhood kids.

"The prostheses I had at that time were sharp. I accidentally fell over one of the youngsters, ripping open the child's leg. He had to have twenty stitches in that leg. I had no business doing such a stupid thing. My actions resulted in unnecessary misery for another individual. It seemed important to me to show those kids I could play soccer—and that I wasn't totally helpless.

"But I shouldn't have done it. Because I was going through

an elementary phase of rehabilitation, I wasn't aware of the damage that could be inflicted by my mechanical fingers. I haven't given up soccer entirely, but when I do play, *I* don't have the freedom to go all out for the win."

A girl in front of Claire whispered to a companion, "That's a phony hand on his left arm, too. Doesn't that give you chills?"

Claire pressed her fingers hard against her eyes, the girl's words reverberating through her brain. She swallowed several times before looking back up at Nick.

"Most of the inmates in my prison are infantile, with little self-control and little recognition of someone else's needs or emotions."

He proceeded to discuss, in the nomenclature of sociology, specific case histories from his experience, of egocentric immaturity that resulted in violence.

"Regrettably, as long as inflamed or disturbed citizens commit mayhem in our communities, penitentiaries will be needed. But I firmly believe that, in the future, we won't need so many of them as we have now."

None of the other men had expressed this opinion. Claire was surprised Nick did. He went on to describe the progress made in counseling, reading instruction, job training, prisoner rehab, and limited access to guns.

"Also, in the next decade," he announced, "medicine will win victories in treating brain injuries, birth defects, malnutrition, alcoholism, and drug addiction."

His tone became pensive. "Modern technology has allowed us to place human beings into compounds of isolation, with supervision now possible from safe distances—well-insulated cubicles down the hall, or even down the *hill*.

"Meals can be dispensed through machines similar to the ones here on campus in dorms. Some of this food may be better fare than what you have dished out in the university dining hall."

He grinned at the groans this remark generated. But the students quieted down quickly as he continued. "Machines are cost-effective. But isn't it pathetic when an inmate survives in a moonscape world alone, or one shared only by individuals just as unprincipled as himself?"

He paused, his head bent down. When he raised it, his eyes seemed to peer over and out beyond the students. Deep in thought, he proceeded, "I hope the inmate of the future will come to appreciate the few decent individuals who bother to enter his world—be they counselors, chaplains, teachers, medics, or even dour-faced superintendents of security like myself. If he doesn't, insanity, more than likely, will be the alternative."

Nick's voice echoed through a quiet room where no coughs or scraping of chairs could be heard at all.

"No, physical plants will not do the job of caring for prisoners adequately," he said. "*People,* with God's guidance, always must be in the forefront of appropriate incarceration policy. Corrections personnel must never allow themselves to be so hardened by the very real violence of the surroundings that they forget that some noble men and women have been unjustly imprisoned over the centuries—Gandhi, Joan of Arc, Martin Luther King, Jesus Christ, to name a few. Nobility of character *can* and often does exist in bondage and chains— even today.

"In summation, as we go about the very necessary task of shutting men and women away from society, we must be careful we don't shut them off from the pathway that leads to their own soul and the destiny possible for that soul."

He ended his statement in a subdued tone. For a second or two there was no response.

Then wild applause erupted.

Hands went up all over the room—healthy, strong young hands, Claire noted. What did Nick think when he saw so many hands raised up before him? His face betrayed no distress.

Afterward, the students thronged the dais. Nick was explaining something to a muscular African-American student as Claire headed into the crowded aisle.

It would be better, she reasoned, if she just spoke to Nick before he saw her, because surely he wouldn't be comfortable knowing she'd held back, gawking at close range. It'd be better to rush right up. That's what she would do if she'd known all along he was an amputee.

She raised her chin, bit her lip just once, and then found some deep reservoir of strength that propelled her forward. She went up the steps onto the dais.

In that instant, Nick glanced her way. She waved, then hurried right up to him. "Your presentation was superb. Where do we line up to vote for you for president, Mr. Van Vierssen?"

He walked around the table and came forward eagerly, his eyes warmly receptive. "Claire, what a nice surprise," he said. "Do you mean to tell me you sat through this whole spiel?"

"Every minute of it." She tried to concentrate on his eyes and avoid looking at the Greifer prosthesis. "And I'm more impressed with you, sir, than you ever could have been with me."

She was relieved he didn't offer the Greifer to shake, or touch her in any way with either prosthesis.

"Impossible."

"Not really, because you'd been to concerts, whereas I had never explored the complexities of prison wardening. To learn there are men like you on this planet, delivering speeches with such expertise and élan—well, that impresses me no end."

"Thank you, maestra," he said with a grin.

She hesitated before blurting out the obvious. "Why didn't you tell me you were coming up to State? Or shouldn't I ask?"

He tilted his head in a paternal manner. "You shouldn't ask."

"I spent two rather miserable evenings trying to come up with a reason why you hadn't mentioned the conference in your letter. I couldn't remember doing or saying anything obnoxious to you. Was there something I did or said or wrote that—"

"No, no. Don't consider such things."

"It's put me in an awkward spot, Nick, because when Jim Gleason learned I wanted to attend the seminar, he invited me to his open house, and frankly, I didn't know how to reply."

"Claire," he replied slowly, his eyes narrowing in thought, "I nearly phoned you. One night soon after I received your CD, I lifted the phone to do just that. I desperately wanted to talk to you."

He spoke hesitantly, as if he wasn't sure how to proceed. He folded his arms across his chest in a way that caused a barely discernible clink—something other than flesh against flesh.

Then, slowly, he moved those arms behind his back, out of sight.

"After a great deal of soul-searching," he continued, "I decided I better not call. I figured that, as a pianist, if you learned I was an amputee, it would make you uneasy in my presence—much more so than it would most people. That's the reason I didn't phone, or drop by your house when I arrived on campus this trip. It's that simple. You mustn't think you said or did anything thoughtless or rude. Quite the contrary. But you fooled me; I worked overtime trying to conceal my handicap from you. I was sure you didn't know about it."

She paused a second. His candor and deep eye contact disarmed her. Nevertheless, she felt satisfied with her performance. She had succeeded in deceiving him up to that point. "Well, I do—I do know. I've known a long time."

"You knew in the city? The night of the recital?"

"I suspected from the first," she offered. "Anyway, didn't you think that I'd learn about it when you came here for the conference?"

"I didn't know *what* I was going to do if you saw me here. On this enormous campus, I figured there was a good chance you wouldn't be aware of the events scheduled by the sociology department. But I obviously was off base on all counts. Things have turned out perfectly."

His cerulean eyes were penetrating hers like X-rays. Knowing of his strong Christian convictions, she felt particularly sinful, resorting to falsehood. But she could see, by the relaxed lines of his mouth, that he was happy it had turned out the way it did.

"So you knew about my disability all along," he said, "and it doesn't matter that much. Is that right?"

"Of course it matters," she replied cautiously, with a bit more confidence. "I guess it's my opinion that any guy who can control stockades full of rapacious prisoners has everything together, ah, hands or no hands."

"Not quite *everything* together, Claire, but—"

"Hey, you two," called Jim, coming toward them. "We're all going on over to the house now. Are you ready to join us?"

"Yes, I think we are," said Nick, accepting the invitation for her. "I'm so pleased to see Claire, Jim. Did she tell you how we met?"

"Yes—unreal! What I want to know, Nick, old buddy, is how you could have encountered such a magnificent female and avoided locking her up in a tower for safe keeping."

"That entered my mind," replied Nick, his chin crinkling in an amused manner.

"I've got to run on ahead to check on the others," Jim added as he backed toward a side door. "Peg's going to be furious that we're late."

He hurried out the door to the coatroom.

The students had gone. Claire and Nick were alone.

With the metal prosthesis, Nick picked up the briefcase in a casual way. But it took heroic self-control on Claire's part to conceal her revulsion. For a second, she steadied herself against the table.

As they headed for the coatroom, she racked her brain to come up with nonsense chatter to relax herself.

"Careful, Nick. I could end up stealing that briefcase again, if you don't watch out. This time I might blackmail you."

"And what nefarious terms would you demand for its safe return?" he asked, his eyes glinting in fabricated terror.

He put his "hand" prosthesis against her back as they

walked through the open doorway into the coatroom. It was comforting to have his arm there, more comfortable than she'd thought it would be with the artificial hand.

"Oh, I might blackmail you by demanding a ski trip to Vail."

"So, Jim told you I ski," he responded, putting down his briefcase and taking his coat, a well-tailored camel's hair, from a coatrack. She couldn't decide whether to help him or not. In those few moments of indecision, he had thrown the coat around himself and was getting into it, awkwardly for sure, but with his own inimitable savoir-faire.

"Jim said you're a sensational skier," she commented, slipping into her own coat.

"Hardly sensational," he said as they went out the side door of the building. "Suffice it to say, I manage to get to the bottom of the mountain most of the time."

They descended the steps, his artificial hand now resting gently on her shoulder. It was a brisk evening, an apple-pie moon emerging over the trees. She was ecstatic to be sharing it with this marvelous man, whose friendship she now valued more than a Telemann fugue or a Beethoven sonata. And for a musician, that was dangerously close to adoration.

"Have you ever skied?" he asked.

"Everyone who's ever lived in Switzerland skis—at least a little bit."

"And you lived in Switzerland?"

"Yes, when I was a youngster. Eventually my music took precedence over skiing, and just about everything else."

"It would have to. Downhill skiing would be too hazardous for you now. If you broke your wrist, you wouldn't be able to honor your contracts. And that would be little short of a disaster."

It was beyond comprehension that they could be talking about broken wrists and piano recitals with such nonchalance. She managed to continue with an almost incoherent, "Yes, I'm sure it would."

"You'll have to stick to watching characters like me out there on the runs. It's no catastrophe if I break my shoulder or arm. I can still function with a cast—at least for a few weeks. I've done such a job on this old body that a broken arm isn't going to be the end of the world. But for you, it'd be a different story entirely. Why don't you blackmail me with something else?"

"All right, but I'd still love to see you outfitted for the slopes, goggles and all. Jim says you even do some jumping."

He laughed. "If the visibility's about five hundred miles. Jim's house is down this street to the right."

"I have a vague idea where it is. I've seen him pulling in and out of the driveway. He always waves."

"I'm sure he does. So, how's the semester going for you? Will your recitals cut into your teaching heavily?"

"No. The only remaining performances are at the beginning of the second semester in January. I'm playing the Schumann A-Minor in Nashville and New Orleans."

"That means a lot of work."

"A busy Christmas vacation, yes."

"No time for caroling. . .or sitting on Santa's knees," he stated bewitchingly.

She laughed. "Actually, I'll be relieved when this season's over. It's been too demanding, though there were highlights. Cincinnati was close to perfection. I was able to perform everything just the way I had always dreamed I could. . . . Oh, I shouldn't go on like this. It's so silly to. . ."

"No, no, I want to hear all about it. But I warn you, you're never going to convince me that anything you played in Cincinnati could top the selections I heard that night in New York.

"Everything was better—better, in fact, than on your CD."

As the wind picked up, he pressed his prosthesis against her shoulder and brought her closer. Once again, she was struck by the fact that she'd been rambling on about her keyboard accomplishments, and for several moments she'd all but forgotten that Nick was without hands.

Yet even being aware of this, she found herself as eager to share her experiences and thoughts with him as she'd been that afternoon at the Lincoln Center.

Why is that? she wondered.

Immediately she answered her own question—Nick came back with caring, appropriate statements that proved his interest. Somehow, she felt compelled to confide her anxieties about her performances following Cincinnati. "The devastating thing is that I'll never have a recital like Cincinnati again."

"Nonsense, of course you will."

"I really doubt it. A 'Cincinnati' comes along very seldom in a career—sometimes only once. Sometimes never. And, Nick, the frustrations of pitting oneself against that one great performance are maddening. The practice needed to reach that pinnacle a second time looms oppressively on the horizon."

He patted her shoulder. "Don't be discouraged by things like that, Claire. Your performance in any city will be a winner. I can see, though, that we both could write books about frustrations, couldn't we?"

He coughed before he replied. "How many hundreds of 'one more times' have we faced, conquering some infinitesimal detail? But because we've been willing to go the distance that hundredth time, we've had successes in ways we never would have thought possible. That's a blessing. It toughens us for that next 'one more time' we may well face tomorrow—if things run true to form."

"Or the 'one more time' we might face tonight?" she found herself asking.

"Possibly even the 'one more time' we could face tonight, yes," he added in a tone of gentle reassurance.

seven

They crossed the street in front of Jim's house. The door was open and music, blending with laughter and conversation, floated out invitingly into the night air. Claire could see Jim's silhouette in the doorway.

Jim called out to them. "Get in here, you two. I was ready to send out the gendarmes."

He took Nick's briefcase, helped them remove their coats, and led them to the living room, where a group of about thirty people were enjoying each other's company.

Peg approached with a tray of stuffed popovers.

"How did it go, Nick?" she asked in the concerned voice of someone who knew him like family.

"Fair enough, Peg," he answered. "We didn't have to use bullhorns to get attention as we do sometimes in the prison yard, so that was encouraging. Peg, you know Claire, I'm sure."

"Of course. I'm so glad you could come, Claire. Would either of you care for an hors d'oeuvre? My *pièce de resistance*—popovers with shrimp."

Claire took one. "They look scrumptious."

"Nick?" Peg offered.

"I'd rather not, thanks," he said, almost as an aside, denoting an understanding between them.

"Oh, Nick, I forgot," said Peg in painful embarrassment. "These kinds of things are so—oh, I'm so sorry. Forgive me. There's roast beef, ham, plates and forks, and a lot of other things on the table. . . ."

"I don't need anything right now, Peg," he said, waving his simulated hand with an easy air. "And don't think any more about it, please. I'll get some ham later."

Claire felt a shudder surge through her. She tried frantically to hide it. The popovers, stuffed to overflowing with shrimp, were undoubtedly too gooey for Nick to manage well.

For a few moments, amid the pleasant din of the crowd, she'd forgotten again about Nick's horrible disability. But *he* could never forget. For him it was always there.

In her distress, she could barely chew the popover. Fortunately, Peg was still talking to Nick. They didn't notice her discomfort.

"How 'bout a glass of punch?" asked Peg.

"Wonderful," Nick replied enthusiastically. "Claire, would you care for punch?"

She nodded, and was able to add a mumbled "Yes, thanks," as she swallowed the last of the popover.

Peg directed them to a table in the library.

It was a convivial crowd, a large number of the guests young marrieds who traveled the byways of the campus with a retinue of children and bouncy dogs. They were eager to talk with Nick and appeared overjoyed to have Claire in their midst.

Here and there were maverick personalities like Tina Gutierrez from the Spanish department, who chattered up a storm with the folks around her. Excited about meeting Nick, Tina introduced him to her boyfriend, a state policeman who had escorted prisoners to Everettsville several times.

Guest lecturers Schwartz and Fillmore had brought their wives along on the trip. Mrs. Schwartz, a smartly dressed woman, outgoing and assertive, seemed particularly excited to learn Claire was from Switzerland.

"Don't you just love the Meinholtz Emporium in Berne?" she asked.

Claire had to confess that she wasn't familiar with the Meinholtz Emporium.

Arnold Saxby had been to Claire's recital in September. He admitted he was flabbergasted to see her at the party, incredulous that she had "condescended" to participate in such a "mundane" gathering.

He managed to get her alone in a corner of the dining room.

"How could a sophisticated woman like you be interested in prisons?" he asked.

"I wasn't—until I met Nick."

"Oh, yes, of course. . .you and Nick are friends."

"Actually, we've known each other only a short time."

"Doesn't it give Nick some qualms to be friends with a girl who has such accomplished—"

"Fingers?"

"Yeah."

How could she get through this evening, Claire wondered, if she had to respond to questions as penetrating as this one? What did she really know about Nick and his qualms? Or about Nick in any regard?

Frantic words tumbled from her mouth. She hoped they made sense. "If he had qualms about me, he'd also have qualms about friends who are baseball players or surgeons. If he hadn't conquered his, er, qualms—he wouldn't have any friends at all."

Arnold raised his eyebrows and nodded. "I'm sure you're right. And he has legions of friends. Was he at your recital in New York, too?"

"Yes."

"Your performance was incredible. Pardon me for asking, but you and Nick—surely, you and Nick aren't. . .serious, are you?"

Another powerhouse question.

Serious? What kind of relationship *did* she have with Nick? She couldn't answer that question for herself, let alone for Arnold Saxby.

Might she become serious with Nick someday? Her gaze sped across the dining room to the library, where he was standing so tall and self-possessed in a group with Tina Gutierrez; he was still very much the Annapolis midshipman.

"Well, what about it?" Arnold continued, pressing a bit too hard.

She paused, trying to pry an intelligent response from her brain. "Nick and I do have mutual interests, but—"

"It'd be tough to plan much of a future with him," Arnold commented. "I mean. . .his handicap's a big thing to overcome."

"It would be, yes."

"In addition, he's got this hang-up about a God-mandated commitment to inmates. Nothing more seems to be on his agenda. Nick's a great guy; no question about that. I wish him the best. But, frankly, if I were a woman, I'd keep my distance."

She nodded, knowing that keeping her distance from Nick was exactly what she had wanted to do earlier that day.

"Anyway," he went on, "if things don't work out with you and Nick, and you're still turned on by jailers, why don't you look me up?" He handed her his card.

With a half-smile, she thanked him and put his card in her skirt pocket.

"I never thought I'd actually envy Nick Van Vierssen," said Arnold, "but right now I sure do. You are a desirable woman."

She touched his arm kindly. Then, realizing she now needed the safe harbor of Nick's presence, she moved toward the library. In addition, a jealousy had crept in as she watched Nick with Tina and the others. She was missing everything he was saying. And because her own time with him was so valuable, she resented others monopolizing him.

Even from the dining room she could hear Tina gushing about something. "That's amazing," she was spouting in her high-spirited voice.

As she moved closer, Claire noticed to her horror, Nick was removing his jacket so Tina could examine the artificial hand attached to his left arm. Apparently not embarrassed, he pushed up his sleeve to show her where some sort of battery was located.

Claire pressed a knuckle hard against her teeth. Tina infuriated her—such a nosy and insensitive woman, pestering Nick about the workings of that grotesque device. How could Tina touch it without recoiling?

Appalled with herself, Claire realized that she, too, was curious. She wanted to know how Nick's prostheses worked, but it jarred her to observe Tina's ease and open curiosity with Nick's accouterments.

Claire studied the demonstration from a few feet away, unobserved by Nick.

"There are small myoelectric signals in the muscles of my arms, Tina," Nick was explaining, "that control the opening and closing of my apparatus. They're pretty weak, for sure. But powered by a small battery here on my arm, this mechanism can pick up these signals on the skin surface and amplify them several hundred thousand times, causing a type of muscle interaction that allows the artificial hand or the prehensile Greifer to move like a normal hand. Well, almost. . ."

He lowered his head a bit before adding, "but not quite."

"That's phenomenal," Tina exclaimed as the rest of the group watched intently.

"The simulated hand looks a lot better, right? But I don't have the dexterity with that which I have with the Greifer." He was now demonstrating the prosthesis on his right hand. "Here you can see the movements more clearly."

Tina was handling the prosthesis. "What a remarkable invention," she commented.

"It's done wonders for me," he continued. "But often I have to revert back to a hooklike unit at the prison, where appearance is less important than functionality. I seldom use the simulated hand while on duty."

Claire felt an arm around her waist. She turned and looked into Jim's comforting countenance.

"Do you think you should be watching this?" he whispered.

She began to shake, but his arm held her steady. "I think it's something I *have* to do, Jim," she replied, her mouth barely shaping the words. "I'll have to try to be more like Tina if I'm to. . ."

"Give me a break. The day you behave like Tina, I'll personally give you a sound thrashing," he said playfully.

"She's not upset at all. Oh, Jim, how can Nick demonstrate those awful things?"

"He knows people have a natural curiosity, so he doesn't mind demonstrating his equipment. After a time, these demonstrations won't upset you, either."

She shook her head doubtfully.

"Be patient with yourself. This has been a rough day. You sure came through tonight, Claire—Nick's happy you're here. From the look of things, I think more than a briefcase passed between the two of you."

They moved nearer Nick. With the help of the state trooper, he had put on his jacket and was taking a slow sip of punch, the demonstration over.

Tina was talking to someone else as Nick polished off the rest of his punch.

But she abruptly turned back to him. "Man," she blurted, "how long did it take you to learn how to do that, Nick—to drink from a punch cup?"

He shrugged his shoulder and answered her in the same patient fashion. "I can't say, Tina. You learn a lot of things simultaneously. I suppose it took a half hour, after months of exercise and practicing with basics. I can't say for sure."

As he spoke, he turned his head a little to the side and noticed Claire. "Oh, there you are, Claire. I wondered what had happened to you."

With soothing eye contact, Claire conveyed a compassion she thought Nick needed after the performance he'd just given.

"Tina," he continued, "like myself, Claire's an old hand at practice that achieves what seems to be the impossible. I bet once in a while she's had to practice three or four weeks on two pages of a Bach fugue. You might say Claire and I represent the poles of manual dexterity. For her it's an accomplishment to play the presto section in that fugue. For me, it's picking up a punch cup. Most of the rest of you fall somewhere between the two of us."

The seconds that followed these words were awkward—nobody appeared to know how to reply to such a profound remark. Even Tina appeared at a loss for words. But Nick had spoken with no perceivable bitterness.

Claire found herself grabbing his right arm, clasping it tightly for strength, feeling the taut biceps below his shoulder. She knew she had to speak—to rescue him and the others from the stalled conversation.

"Nick may fall short of my mark in manual dexterity," she managed, "but he can outski most of us. On those slopes his legs more than make up for his manual deficiency."

"No fooling," said Craig, an instructor from the physics department. "Now you're talking *my* language."

"He's even done some jumping," Claire added.

"Wait a minute. Hold everything." Shaking his head, Nick grinned at Craig. "With my disability, I can only tackle the most innocent trails. No slalom. But yes, I do jump, though I probably shouldn't. It's kamikaze-time when I take off."

"I tried jumping once, Van Vierssen," said Craig. "It scared the pants off me."

Nick laughed. "It's supposed to. But after you get the hang of it, it's not that hard. Downhill can be just as dangerous."

Craig wanted to know where Nick skied. They compared notes, then decided they'd have to plan a trip together. "Be sure to wear suspenders for your pants," Nick joked.

The party didn't wind down till nearly one o'clock. After the others had left, Nick volunteered his and Claire's services to help the Gleasons pick up. Then he offered to escort Claire home.

Jim walked out to the porch with them. He patted Claire on the shoulder. "It was great you could make it, Claire. Stop in again—and soon."

"I will, Jim, and. . .thanks—thanks for inviting me." She spoke the words slowly, hoping Jim would read into them the deep appreciation she had for his encouragement throughout the traumatic hours of the most soul-searching day of her life.

Though the air was a bit colder than it had been when they'd come from the Student Union, it was still comfortable enough for Claire to take pleasure in the short stroll.

"It may be a bit too windy to cross the parade grounds," she said. "Do you mind if we go down Chestnut Street and around?"

"That's fine," Nick replied. "I marched across enough windy parade grounds and football fields when I was at the Naval Academy to last me a lifetime."

She wasn't prepared for this reference to his naval career because of the reason it had been cut short. A garbled reply was all she could come up with as they started up the sidewalk.

"Oh, I guess you didn't know I went to Annapolis?"

"Ah—er, yes, Jim told me."

"I thought he probably had."

She hoped he wouldn't pursue this subject. She had prepared no script for discussing the trauma he'd experienced during this phase of his life.

But he went on with no hesitation whatsoever. "It was the third summer I was a midshipman that I sustained the injury that took my hands. So parade grounds don't conjure up many happy memories, Claire."

"I can see why," she gulped, deciding to change the subject immediately. "Nice party, wasn't it?"

"Yes. I'm glad you were there. Peg and Jim are terrific people, and so are their kids. Do you know their children?"

"No, I really don't."

"They were farmed out tonight, with neighbors. But you'll have to meet them. Todd's the best swimmer—he's won a lot of ribbons."

"They have three children, right?"

"Yes, but Jim told me tonight that Peg's expecting another."

"That'll be a houseful. How will they ever manage?"

Nick shook his head. "I haven't the foggiest idea. They both come from large families, though. I guess that prepares a couple for an onslaught of little ones. I'm an only child myself. What about you, Claire?"

"I'm an 'only,' too. My parents were middle-aged when they married—my mother was a petite Swiss woman, delicate like a Spanish figurine. She died when I was five, so I have only sketchy memories of her; none of them suggest she was ever frazzled with the care of an infant."

"But she was. And from my observation, her efforts paid off in great style."

Claire laughed. "Thank you. Nevertheless, the fact remains, I have a hard time envisioning my mother as anything but dreamlike. Papa idolized her. He never fully coped with her death. I'm sure he was anxious to join her when he died six years ago."

Nick looked down at her, his eyes in the light of a street lamp projecting deep sadness. "It must be lonely for you sometimes."

"Sometimes, yes. But I have cousins in Boston who are considerate and kind. And, of course, I have Henri Poncelet and his daughter."

"Who exactly are those folks?"

"My dearest friends—more family than friends." Claire indicated a turn away from the parade grounds. "Henri was my father's business partner, but also my 'little uncle.' Before Papa died, he made sure Henri would see to my welfare. Anyway, the Poncelets spoil me fiercely, phoning often, even from Paris.

"Actually, I don't know what I'd do without them. Henri's fanatically French. A lady's man of the first order, so his marriages never last. As a Christian, Papa didn't approve of Henri's cavalier attitude toward marriage. I don't either, but Henri's a good man and tremendously happy."

Nick gave her a questioning look. "Is he? I doubt it. His life sounds like a dismal merry-go-round."

She went on to tell him about some of Henri's outlandish women. "Babette was my favorite. She made mouthwatering crepes."

"Do you think Henri married her just for her crepes?" Nick asked mischievously.

"She *did* have other notable qualities." Claire chuckled, picturing the statuesque Babette. "However, those qualities, even with the crepes, didn't fill the bill. Henri divorced her three years ago."

"It's sad he's never found a lasting relationship. I'm sure he experiences few days of real contentment, despite outward appearances."

They walked on in silence for a few moments, both inhabiting their own thoughts, with Claire focusing on the contrast between Henri and Nick.

Despite their differences, they were exceptional men. She admired them both. She knew they would enjoy each other's company if they ever met.

But Henri didn't have Nick's indomitable fortitude. She had the feeling a handicap like Nick's would have prompted her French uncle to commit suicide.

She scuffed the leaves as they walked, making a scrunching, swishing sound on the sidewalk. Nick kicked up a few also, and they laughed as the leaves took flight into the swirling wind.

She bent down to pick some up, but they were brittle and decaying.

"None of the leaves this late in the year are worth keeping," she commented.

"They've had their day," he responded. "It's on to the next season. I, for one, am looking forward to winter. Time to get out my skis. We can't dwell on the broken leaves of autumn, Claire. You just grind them up and send them on their way."

There were a hundred ways to interpret Nick's words.

What was behind these comments about discarded leaves? Because he was such a new acquaintance, and because he lived with such a horrendous disability, Claire simply didn't have sufficient insight to understand his references to discarded leaves—or anything else.

eight

"Turn left here," Claire said, directing Nick onto Regent Street. "My house is halfway down the block, the one with the light peeking through the wisteria bush. I'll bet you don't have a wisteria bobbing about outside your window at Everettsville."

"I don't have a bush *or* tree within a hundred yards of my window," he replied with humorous emphasis. "But, Claire, my apartment is hardly a cell, even though my address is the prison. I have a nice place, actually."

"No bars on your doors or carbo-whatever windows with electrical impulses to prevent your escape?"

He chuckled a reply. "No. Nothing like that."

"Do all the superintendents live on the grounds?"

"I'm the only one who does. My boss and the rest of the senior staff are married and live in Fulton Falls or Ridglea."

"And you wouldn't rather live in town, too, Nick? Doesn't it get depressing being at the prison all the time?"

"Now and then it does, yes. But I get away, often—to Canada skiing, sometimes to Norfolk to visit my parents, and to assorted locales on lecture tours, like this one. Once in a while I even sneak down to the city and take in a piano recital or two."

The droll tone implied a smile, but it was too dark away from a streetlight for her to notice. His tone became more serious as he went on.

"You have to understand, though, Claire, that living at the prison has advantages for me—advantages over living in town. Every now and then, I can't manage something without assistance—a knot or a latch, for example, or something dumb like that. When that happens, I can call the officer at the desk. He'll send someone over—to give me a hand, literally."

Fortunately, darkness under the trees prevented Nick from noticing the startled pain in her eyes. The details he was relating slashed her mind like so many machetes. Would she ever accept the fact that Nick Van Vierssen—strong, confident, brilliant, sophisticated Nick—was handicapped?

He had accepted this fact, but could she? How many months or years would it take for her to adjust to the fact that this super guy had to live in a place as grim as a prison so he could call upon someone to help him if he couldn't untie a knot?

Unaware of her discomfort, he continued. "I have personnel to clean up the place—to make my bed and do some of those other pesky details. So, you see, my life's pretty soft, after all. I'll bet you had no idea how posh it was to live in a prison."

"No, I never knew it could be so. . .so, ah, comfortable," she replied, amazed she was able to answer him at all.

"I have a closet-sized kitchen, a disorderly bedroom, and a living room knee-deep in books. I have a fine stereo system, a necessity because I receive CDs in the mail now and then from celebrated musicians."

He was in such a good mood, she found her own spirits beginning to perk up. She responded cheerfully, "Well, aren't you the lucky bum?"

"I'd say so. One of my friends is so famous, she has write-ups regularly in the *Times*." He looped his arm through hers and pulled her toward him playfully with the artificial hand, as they turned into her walkway by the wisteria bush.

"You're coming in, aren't you?" she said persuasively, convinced he would.

"I don't think I better, Claire. Do you have any idea how late it is?"

"Who looks at the time? I'm going to have a cup of hot chocolate—top quality, right from Bern. Besides, aren't you just dying to see my plum-colored plant?"

He laughed in resignation. "As a matter of fact, yes, I am. Okay. Hot chocolate would be great."

Unlocking the door that opened into the living room, she

turned on a light on a side table.

"Why, this is a great place, Claire. The modular sofa's right out of Rodeo Drive. Nothing that elegant graces my apartment at Everettsville."

"It's the most expensive thing I ever bought."

He swung off his coat and tossed it over the banister.

"Let me hang that up for you."

"Oh, no. Don't bother." He scanned the room and then burst into laughter. "So there's the plant! I don't believe it. Even Luther Burbank would rave over that specimen."

"Isn't it monstrous?" She tossed her own coat over the sofa. "I'm sure it's some sort of mongrel with the ability to devour me. Who knows?"

"I wouldn't like that to happen," he replied with a theatrical scowl, "although I'm sure even the plant must think of you as a choice morsel." He folded his arms and studied the room further. "You play a little chess, I see."

"Rather poorly. Do you play?"

"I used to be pretty fair, but not many men at Everettsville play chess. Poker is more their speed. . . . Ah, and look at that grand piano—it's magnificent."

"My papa bought it for me when I was thirteen."

"Your father was very supportive, then, of your career?"

"Oh, yes. He was a darling. You and he would have hit it off well. Everyone loved my father—goatherds near our home in Montreux, businessmen in New York where we had an apartment. Papa had genuine respect for everyone. Like you do, Nick."

"Like me?" His eyes narrowed in puzzlement. He wrinkled amused lips as he reached over and put his arm on her shoulder. "Some of the inmates don't think I have much empathy at all, Claire. But thanks for the compliment. I'm honored to be compared to your father."

"He was a Christian, too, as you are," she added. "I liked the way he prayed with me when I was a child. God seemed very close in those days."

"Not in *these* days?"

"Well, not exactly. Although I get to church most Sundays, I've been shortchanging God when it comes to private prayer. Asking God's guidance in my pursuits doesn't pull the weight that it should."

She paused, expecting him to jump right into a Christian platitude, but he didn't. He merely allowed his glance to rest softly on hers, waiting for her to continue. Awkwardly, she headed for the kitchen. "Let me see about getting that cocoa going."

"Good."

She put milk into a saucepan and turned on the stove, while Nick removed mugs from a mug tree. For too long, her eyes concentrated on what he was doing, executed with jerky arm and shoulder movements. She knew he detected her discomfort, but he said nothing.

He suddenly looked startled. Claire noticed the cat had brushed through his legs. "Galuppi's playing London Bridge with you," she remarked, glad to have a cause for a chuckle.

He smiled when he saw it was a cat. He bent down on one knee to stroke Galuppi. "I really like cats, Claire; we have something in common—claws."

Claire all but dropped the chocolate tin she was holding. She recalled he had mentioned a hook prosthesis in his talk that day. Trembling, she set the tin down on the counter. Unable to utter a word, barely able to breathe, she smothered a gasp that almost escaped her chest.

Not at all ill-at-ease, Nick seemed to be getting a kick out of the cat. "How did you choose the name Galuppi?"

She took a deep breath, able to reply, "Baldasare Galuppi was a talented eighteenth-century composer who's pretty much ignored today. The name's always amused me. When this stray feline appeared on the scene, I named him Galuppi after that composer."

He stroked the cat with the Greifer. "It's a sensational name."

"Galuppi likes you. That's unusual. He's a terrible snob."

"Well, I like Galuppi," he said, getting back up on his feet.

She forced a sparkle of sorts into her voice. "Galuppi's had to adjust to a legion of cat sitters. As you know, I'm out of town a lot. Next summer, I'll be in Paris for three months."

"With Henri and—ah, Yolande?"

"Yes."

"You prefer Europe to the States, don't you?"

"Only because my closest friends live in Paris and Switzerland. I haven't many close friends here."

"That surprises me. You're so lovely." He studied her face. "In your dressing room that night at Lincoln Center, you were surrounded by friends, all basking in your success. I just assumed your life was one soiree after another."

He continued, almost sadly. "But I should have remembered, skilled artists like you can't indulge in many soirees. You probably don't have time away from practice for chess, dancing, or much fun at all."

"That's about it. Even on vacation, a day without practice is costly." She poured the cocoa into the mugs.

"Today you were derelict in your duties, spending a good share of it listening to four jokers rant and rave about lockups."

"Yes, but I'm not a bit sorry."

He put a spoon in his mug and lifted it from the counter with both prostheses. So much maneuvering was involved, Claire's uneasiness returned as she watched him. However, he appeared oblivious to this as they went into the living room.

"Don't you yearn sometimes for a release from all the pressure?" he asked. "You're too young to live as a hermit, practicing all the time. I'll wager there are erudite history professors and virile football coaches clamoring at your door while you're practicing all those hundreds of hours. In fact, I bet you had to cancel a date to attend the seminar and party."

He put the mug on the coffee table and sat down on the sofa.

"Actually," she said, sitting next to him, "I hardly sequester myself, Nick. I date often—on weekends—as much as I care to right now."

"Good. I'm relieved to know you're in circulation. I must tell Jim to keep an eye on you."

He bent over and took a spoonful of cocoa. "This *is* good chocolate, Claire. Anyway, as I was saying, Jim better check on you. Music's a noble art, but all of us need an occasional change of pace in our routine, commitment or no commitment."

The joy of relaxing with him had swiftly returned, despite the pain she experienced as she observed his difficulty in drinking from the mug. She was drawn to him by a kind of magnetism. She found she was temporarily able to put his disability aside as they chatted.

"So that's why you ski?"

"Yes—and I like to travel, too. I've been to Paris, myself."

"You're the sly one. Why didn't you say so earlier?"

"No reason to."

"Don't you *love* it?"

"Somewhat, but I prefer Salzburg and Innsbruck."

"Because of the ski slopes?"

"I suppose."

"You'd love Paris, too, if *I* took you around—showed you the delicious nooks and crannies and introduced you to my friends."

"I'd like to think that would make a difference."

"You belong in Europe, Nick, striding up the Place Vendome, or perusing the stock reports over a drink in a café near the Bois. You're so out of place at a prison. How can you stand it?"

"The same way you can stand practicing for hours at your piano. We've found jobs that consume us, Claire, and we're fortunate to have those jobs—at least *I* certainly am. I'm not so comfortable in the cafés in Paris as I am in Everettsville. For me, new situations are often frustrating, *always* embarrassing, and sometimes downright unsafe. I enjoy traveling; don't get me wrong. But it's important for me to have my prison. It's there where I make a difference, and it's there where I'm needed. That's my calling. God wants me there."

"You sincerely believe that?"

"Yes, I do," he answered with conviction.

"God might want you to try something special next summer, though. He might want you to share the sights with me in Paris, now that we've become friends."

He paused before he answered her. "Claire, it's risky for us to think of each other as friends."

"It is? Riskier for us than the rest of mankind?"

"Yes, much more so. We're hardly similar to the rest of mankind. You're a recognized performing artist. I have a debilitating handicap and a job with a great deal of responsibility. We're not careless, frivolous individuals. Perhaps that's why we find each other's company so enjoyable. We've touched each other profoundly, haven't we?"

He cleared his throat as if he were attempting to find the exact words to express his thoughts. "Even the word *touch* has an awesome meaning for us. Touch is taken for granted by most people—but never by you, and most definitely never by me. Claire, it's something both of us weave our dreams around. But we're locked into demanding roles, and without them we'd be lost—bereft of purpose. If we neglected our careers we couldn't live with the guilt, or the—"

"But, Nick, couldn't you and I have these same careers and also find time for a now-and-then type of friendship? You *said* everyone needs an escape."

She clutched his upper right arm, where she knew he would feel the power of her grip. How marvelous it felt to press her fingers into that muscular arm. "Come to Paris next summer, Nick. Visit us in Paris—Henri, Yolande, and me. We'll see that you have all the comforts of. . .ah. . .of prison. And I'll learn how to fix escargot."

He took a deep breath. "I'll consider it, Claire. That's the best I can say."

She forced a smile.

He stood and let her hand slip away. "Claire, it's after two. Hadn't we better say good night?"

"I hate to."

"I know. But you'll be tired tomorrow—not up to the eight hours of practice your schedule calls for."

"I haven't even thought of my schedule tonight."

"But you must. And tomorrow I have to drive back to Everettsville."

He picked up his coat from the banister and maneuvered into it. Though it took great restraint, she refrained from assisting him.

"I'll see you tomorrow before you go, surely," she said.

"No, I don't think so. I'm getting an early start so that I can relieve another guy at one o'clock. I gave my word—he's going to a family reunion."

With great effort, he attempted to open the door. Then he turned to her. "Knowing you has been a fine experience for me, Claire." He put both prostheses around her back. Then he leaned over and kissed her forehead.

Her head fell between the lapels of his overcoat and jacket and rested on his chest, her face enveloped by a musky after-shave. She could almost feel his skin through his shirt.

"You've given me a wonderful evening, honey," he whispered softly down to her. "And I appreciate it—especially because I know how difficult it was for you."

She pulled away in surprise. "It wasn't difficult at all. I loved being with you—every second."

"It *was* difficult because—ah—because you didn't know before today that I was an amputee, did you?"

She staggered back, but he kept her from falling, and as he did, she felt a hard metal prosthesis against her back. He grimaced, knowing it had caught her off guard.

"Jim should never have told you," she said angrily. "It was wrong and cruel of him to—"

"Jim didn't tell me. But I knew. . ."

"All evening. . .you knew?"

"Yes. There was no way you could have found out in the city. You obviously didn't know at the recital. And there were things tonight that gave you away. But Claire, you're a stoic, heroic, and thoughtful person—without exception, the most accomplished and astonishing woman I've ever known."

The tears she had tried so hard to control now cascaded from her eyes. "I was sure I'd fooled you. Oh, Nick, I was so sure. This afternoon when I found out. . .it was. . .it was just so devastating for me. I didn't want to lie to you, but I felt I had to. It was all I could do to go to Jim's open house. Nick, I've never faced anything so. . ."

"Don't cry—please. The evening's been such a winner. But it was important that I tell you I knew—things should be out in the open between us, Claire. Besides, I had to express how profoundly moved I've been this evening by your restraint and your most successful attempt to make me feel comfortable. You've been extremely considerate of my feelings. That means a lot to me. Thank you so much."

Impulse got the better of her. She pulled his face down to hers, and pressed her cheek against his. "Nick, don't just walk away again as you did in the city. Please don't. Your being an amputee doesn't matter a bit. Consider a little escape kind of friendship with me. Nothing more. Call me next week. . . ." The tears flowed down both her cheeks.

He held her tight. Then his lips found hers. And they were experienced lips, lips that had kissed women passionately before. If not recently, at one time, certainly. In his kiss there was desperate urgency that gripped her whole being. He released her slowly, kissing her hair in a gesture of farewell.

"You'll call, Nick? And come back soon?" she pleaded, almost in a gasp, still breathing heavily from the overwhelming pressure of his lips.

He answered only with a few slow nods. Then he was out the door and down the path.

He waved as he crossed the street into the wind. The gusts had picked up velocity and swirled bitingly against her face, forcing her to close the door.

Something extraordinary had happened to both of them, she

knew. His kiss had made that obvious. Yet he was not coming back. He wouldn't return, she was sure, despite the powerful attraction they shared. She knew he would be steeling himself against this love he had not bargained for, a love that had popped into his monastic life like a jack-in-the-box.

And it had been the same for her. She hadn't expected anything like this to show up on *her* packed agenda.

Yet, here indeed was a man to whom she *could* commit for a lifetime.

Was the *"Pere éternel,"* the "Eternal Father" who Nick honored so completely, working behind the scenes, calling such strange plays as briefcase exchanges for Nick and herself?

It seemed that might be true.

She fell back against the wall, pressing her fingers to her eyes. "Oh, God, on the chance that You're out there listening, I appeal to You. You know how much that sensational man deserves joy and happiness in his life. I pray—yes, Lord, I *do* pray—that if You've chosen me to be the agent of his happiness, You will show me how to bring it about."

She brushed her hair back from her face, her tears drying salty against her cheeks, as she remembered to add, "in Jesus' name."

nine

At first, Claire had clung to a glimmer of hope that Nick would drop her a line. But that glimmer faded as the days marched drearily onward.

Jim and Peg had become close friends of Claire since their party in the fall. Claire loved their darling children and enjoyed picking out Christmas gifts for them.

On New Year's Day, she stopped by the Gleasons' for a brief visit. The children eagerly showed her their presents, many still under the tree. Claire felt an anguished joy handling the gifts that had come from Nick—adorable puppets for the girls and a spaceship for Todd. As Claire fondled these toys, it was as if a bit of Nick was with her, sharing the holiday spirit.

She'd sent him a card. It had taken her hours to find one, yet it barely skimmed the surface of her feelings. When she tried to add a personal message, she couldn't think of anything appropriate to say.

It was excruciating to know that, even though Nick had displayed incredibly deep feelings for her, she would not see him again. The leaves of their moments together had become brittle, only to be pulverized and tossed into the swirling wind of memory.

His card to her had arrived in mid-December, the day after she'd sent hers, so she realized with some satisfaction that his card was not a response to the one she had sent. It was a well-designed card featuring the three wise kings; it was simply signed "Nick."

The only thing she could hang onto was the fact that the "k" in his name had an excessively long tail, as if he hadn't wanted to lift the pen from the paper, that he, too, had wanted to write something more, but couldn't.

When she got on the plane to fly south for her two concerts, she felt no enthusiasm whatsoever. Her brilliant career had become merely a job.

❧

The morning after her return to campus, as Claire headed across the parade grounds, she heard Jim Gleason's voice ringing out from the steps of the arts building. It lifted her spirits, and she managed a smile and a wave.

He hurried down to her. "Wait a minute," he called, explaining he'd seen her from his office window. He was without a jacket, rubbing his arms in the chilly morning air. "I tried to get you on the phone—the baby came early this morning."

"Oh, Jim, I'm so glad. Tell me, was the sonogram accurate? Was it a boy?"

"Oh, yes, a hearty boy. His name's Josh. Peg's fine. She'll be home tomorrow."

"So soon?"

"They don't pamper mothers in hospitals anymore. It's in and out, so they can return to the spinning wheel and butter churn where they belong."

Claire laughed. "I'll get over to the house soon to see Peg and Josh. Is there anything I can do? I've been rather a fair-weather friend, but maybe I can make up for lost time. The past few weeks have been so. . ."

"You look ragged out, Claire. Are you well?"

"I'll make it."

"You should have devoured more grits down south. Survival in the bayous requires the consumption of a platter of grits and chitlins every morning."

"Now he tells me. In any event, I'm sure I'll outlive you—especially if you stay out in your shirtsleeves."

He rubbed his arms more vigorously. "Could you step into the building for a minute? There's something I want to discuss with you."

"It's like this. . . ," he said with some embarrassment as they sat down in his office. "Nick phoned last week—about a possible field trip for my students through the new building at Everettsville. I thought it only fair to tell you—in case you'd like to go along."

"That's considerate of you, Jim," she answered slowly, her feelings halfway between jubilation and grave apprehension. "Did Nick invite me?"

"No—no, he didn't. And it's stupid, because he's crazy about you. He always asks what you're doing when he calls. This time was no exception. He was hoping all was going well with your concert tour."

"But he didn't ask me to join the field trip?"

"No."

"And you didn't tell him you were thinking of asking me?"

"I didn't, no, because—"

"Jim, I couldn't just breeze down there without telling him."

"No, you can't. It's not permitted, in fact. I have to fax the names ahead of time so they can run security checks." Jim shook his head. "I just thought, once Nick sees you again, he'll realize what a bozo he is. If he *doesn't* want you there— well, once he gets the list, he can phone us and say so. That's the way I see it. Do you think you'd like to go?"

She interlaced her fingers tightly before replying. "I'd give anything to see him again. You know that. When is this field trip scheduled?"

"March 26. It's a Saturday."

"I'm free that weekend, so, ah—do you need an extra car?"

"We might. Yes, I think we will." He folded his arms and stared into her eyes. "Claire, this whole Nick-thing is so rough on you. I wish I could. . ."

"Yes, it's rough. But I make sure I'm terribly busy. In June I'm going to Paris. Maybe I can get myself back on keel over there. It doesn't make much sense for a man to affect me as Nick has. I barely know the guy."

"Sometimes that's the way it happens, though. You meet someone and life does an about-face."

"Apparently, that's what *did* happen to me." She paused in

thought for a moment, then added, "Jim, do you think Nick's handicap is so devastating that he and I couldn't get around it somehow, at least as friends?"

"Frankly, it's not within my power to understand his situation, even though he's discussed it with me a good bit," Jim said, tapping his mouse pad. "But more and more lately, a vivid and most unpleasant scene comes to mind. I walked in on Nick once when he didn't have his prostheses on. He was getting out of bed in a hotel room when I popped in. His door was open, and. . ."

"And?"

"It shook me up. I've got to admit, it did shake me up."

"So we're not dealing with a pair of glasses here, after all, are we? And we never were."

"No, we're not, Claire. I played things down to help Nick have fun the night of the open house, having no idea how much you cared for him. Since that night, Peg and I have considered you as a good friend, too. Your feelings matter to us as much as Nick's."

Jim got up and put a hand on her shoulder. "Peg and I have prayed about your situation because seeing this relationship between the two of you fizzle saddens us—especially when you're both so miserable alone. For my money, that briefcase episode was arranged by the Holy Spirit to bring together two remarkable human beings."

"I'd love to believe that, Jim. It's a big step for me to embrace a faith that accepts God working in one's life, but I'm reading the Bible regularly, trying to take that step. I'll try to convince myself this excursion to Everettsville is part of God's plan."

"Let's just declare it *is,* and let God take it from there, while we. . ."

The buzzer for class muffled Jim's words.

"I have to run, Claire," he declared. "I'll give you a call when we have all the details firmed up about the field trip."

"Fine. And, Jim, I'll stop over in a few days to see Peg."

He squeezed her arm gently as they walked toward the door. "Wait till you get a load of that baby. A real winner. The spittin' image of the old man."

Claire grinned as she watched Jim bound down the stairs to class.

♪

A few weeks later, Jim phoned. "All systems are go, Claire. You're on the list—signed, sealed, and approved. The letter came from Nick's office, so he must have seen your name."

"You're sure, now?"

"Yup—you're on board, lady. And by the way, we can use your car if the offer still holds."

"It does."

"Good. Front of Old Main—nine o'clock—and wear something subdued, like cotton baseball sweats. There are guidelines here: no peekaboo nylon thingie. All females are to be swaddled in flannel like they've spent the winter in bed with the croup. That's the mandate from your sanctimonious friend, Van Vierssen."

She giggled. "Nick's not quite that sanctimonious. Seriously, what should I wear?"

"The actual guidelines are as follows: 'Improperly clothed females will be prevented from touring the grounds.' "

Despite her mixed feelings about the pending excursion, she had to burst out laughing. "I'll scrounge up a potato sack somewhere."

"Perfect," he chortled.

♪

The day of the outing, she settled on a denim skirt and a beige sweater set. Rather than putting her hair up in a chignon, she allowed it to fall softly to her shoulders so she'd more readily blend in with the students. She splashed on only a hint of cologne.

She pulled up into the caravan in front of Old Main at 8:30, and the four waiting students piled in.

For a while she chatted with them. But as they got closer to

Everettsville, she became more detached. None of the kids seemed to share her anxiety about visiting a maximum security prison.

From the bluff of a hill, she got her first view of the compound. Though illuminated by the brilliant shafts of a warm sun, the buildings below remained cold, almost menacing. It was a vast reservation, as large as the university. Patrol towers erupted from numerous corners of the dozen or so three-story-tall peripheral buildings.

Two rows of high fencing topped with twisted loops of barbed wire—which resembled, in supreme irony, a Slinky toy—snaked around the vast compound, up beyond a knoll to a far horizon. Inside the fencing, nearest the highway, stood a sizable new building of gray concrete.

But even with its spanking new walls and roof, it looked austere against the stark landscape, bereft of foliage so early in the spring. What few trees there were on the grounds looked pathetic in their leafless state.

It was inconceivable to Claire that Nick could inhabit such a place. Nicks of the world belonged at Wimbleton or Hilton Head for Renaissance Weekend, consorting with the jet set, not here on this remote hillside, behind barbed wire, in the company of felons.

Jim led the group—which numbered about forty individuals—into a small building on the edge of the lot. Holding the door for them, he followed Claire and the students into the reception room: a nondescript place with brown plastic furniture and a utilitarian, amber-colored carpet.

Jim spoke with a female receptionist, and she picked up a phone to punch a number.

"Mr. Van Vierssen will be here in a few minutes," Jim announced to the students, as he took a pile of papers from the counter. "I'm passing around some instruction sheets for you to read—and heed. Everything written here must be followed to the letter. Such tours as this are rare. Your safety depends on the respect you pay to the instructions on these sheets."

The papers were passed throughout the group, and Claire glanced at the outline in a cursory manner. How could she concentrate on printed matter when in the next instant Nick would walk through the double doors by the counter?

Faintly she heard an outer door bang shut. Then the doors in front of them swung open automatically. There he was— the tall, commanding presence of him! The Nick of her every waking thought.

To her regret, the dim lights of the room showed no particular interest in highlighting his goldenrod hair, which seemed more carefully combed than at the university. His cheeks had no crinkles of merriment by the eyes. His mouth formed no smile.

Beneath the familiar olive green jacket he'd had on that morning at Lincoln Center, he now wore a stiffly starched white shirt and an austere, striped tie.

On his left arm he had the Greifer prosthesis, on his right, the sharper, clawlike hook he'd mentioned in his talk at the sociology seminar. Claire decided no one would ever wear something so gross unless efficiency—or safety—demanded it.

But the effect was hideous. Nevertheless, the students seemed electrified by his presence. Nobody spoke or moved.

His eyes looked particularly weary as they scanned the room until they found her. Then they paused. Effort twisted his mouth into a bittersweet smile. She found it difficult to respond with a smile of her own. But one did come forth. And she waved her hand a trifle, glad she could at least do that.

He was followed into the room by four men in black trousers and maroon blazers, a uniform of sorts.

When he addressed the students, there was none of the relaxed levity he had displayed at the university.

"We're pleased you have an interest in our new facility. It's state of the art, and we're eager to move in after the dedication ceremonies tomorrow."

Gingerly he slid one of the papers from the pile on the counter, manipulating it from one prosthesis to the other.

Claire gritted her teeth watching the operation, recognizing how difficult it was for him to grasp something as thin as a sheet of paper.

"You have one of these, I trust. I'm going to insist you follow everything scrupulously. This is not a safe place for any of you, least of all you young women."

He allowed one corner of his mouth to relax. "As the instructions state, you're to refrain from conversing with inmates as you walk about. Later in the day, you'll have an opportunity to talk with a group of them in our conference room. You can ask questions freely at that time."

He put the Greifer into the crook of his elbow and the hook from his other arm against his chin. "At no time will you be permitted to wander off on your own. Under *no* circumstances will you accept from or give to an inmate anything at all—not anything! Such action will be justification for your immediate removal from the grounds."

Claire saw that his eyes remained focused on her for the few seconds needed to complete his instructions. "Because I have a meeting, I'll be unable to escort you around this morning. But after lunch, I'll join you in the conference room."

He turned to the men next to him. "These men will be your guides. Mr. Dudley, Mr. Thompson, Mr. Renzi, and Mr. Henson. All are knowledgeable about the entire complex here at Everettsville. Gentlemen, they're all yours."

Mr. Henson stepped forward and announced the procedures for entering through the sally port, instructing them to leave valuables at the desk. "Each of you individually will go through a metal detector, be photographed, and frisked—er, checked over."

He blushed slightly, then continued, "It's only a superficial check. We'll assemble in the yard beyond the far door."

As the students lined up by the sally port, Jim spoke to Nick in muted tones. He put his hand on Nick's arm, said something calming, and they both began to chuckle, after which Jim went on to the sally port.

Nick edged through the crowd toward Claire.

"It's good to see you again," he said, mowing down her composure with his powerful blue eyes, causing a shiver to permeate her entire body. "But this wasn't wise, for many reasons."

She surveyed his face, trying to commit to memory every detail. "It was, ah, too great an opportunity for me to miss, Nick. Jim thought I'd like to check out the prison—*and* you. Since you didn't phone him when you saw my name on the list, he figured you didn't mind my being part of the group. Was he right?"

"Contrary to my better judgment, Claire, I *did* want to see you again. Very much." He hesitated, then added. "You look pale. Galuppi can't be taking very good care of you."

With these words the crow's-feet began to crinkle, and the familiar smile returned to his lips.

"This modern generation of cats has no responsibility at all," she replied, glad he was relaxed enough to discuss Galuppi.

"You've been overdoing, I'm sure, with the concerts in Tennessee and New Orleans."

"I'm glad the tour's over."

"The Schumann Concerto—no problems?"

"No, the orchestras were superb, Nick. You'd have loved the conductor in New Orleans. He was the wildest gnome of a man."

"Is there any chance of my getting another CD? Of *that* performance?"

"It'll be in the mail Monday."

"Great. Jim said you've been back since last month."

"I returned the same day the Gleasons' baby made his appearance."

He grinned as he asked, "Have you seen little Josh?"

"Yes, often. He's darling. It's been far too long since I've been close to an infant, and, well, he's precious—for me a precious novelty."

"I'll have to get up there and look him over."

"You must, yes, and. . ." Suddenly she could no longer look up at him because it upset her so.

"And what?" he asked, raising her chin with his Greifer, forcing her to face him.

"I just wanted to say that if you come up—well, I'm living in the same old place."

He nodded several times, his grin fading. "That's good to know."

She tossed her head a little and changed the subject. "I see most of my group has gone on—I'd better get up there and follow them."

She started toward the sally port, and he followed.

Abruptly, he put his Greifer under her arm and drew her back. "Claire," he said, his eyes riveted on hers, "you're much too attractive for a hole like this. Please be careful. Use extreme caution as you tour the grounds."

"Don't worry about me, Nick. I've hiked through the Red Light district of Paris and the docks in London. I won't swish my skirt an inch, or bat an eye."

"To those men in the cell blocks, you and the other girls are just so many. . ." He mumbled syllables of words she couldn't quite decipher, but only guess at.

As she looked into his eyes, she wondered if he was reading her thoughts, which kept pummeling her brain with the question: *And Nick, what am I to you?*

"Claire," he added, reluctantly letting her go, "don't lower your guard, not for a second. Understand?"

"I understand," she replied, continuing on to the sally port.

ten

The group toured the new unit first. Designed to accommodate several hundred men, the facility featured windows free of bars and steel mesh on the doors. Claire remembered the windows could electronically register attempted escapes. The cells, though small, had nicely painted walls, with furnishings of attractive, durable plastic.

"Hey," said one of the girls as they left the new complex, "those rooms are better than mine at Grainger Hall. I think I'll move down here. My plaid curtains would look great in that pad we just saw."

"But not your teddy bear," chided a quarterback called Bif.

The old cell blocks, however, were another story entirely. Mr. Henson informed the students that, because of the overcrowded conditions, these buildings would continue to be used even after the new complex was opened. Cell block C looked like a scene out of an old flick, the central exercise area echoing shouts, catcalls, and some with obnoxious obscenities from the cells above. Because prisoners had to be locked in their cells when visitors toured, rattling of bars and the banging of metal exacerbated the noise level into a cacophony that jangled the nerves.

Surveillance monitors hung from the ceilings of each room and hallway. Uniformed guards, a few of them women, roamed the halls watchfully at frequent intervals.

The halls seemed to go on forever. The din hammered into Claire's skull until she trembled, realizing only too well that unhealthy overcrowding existed throughout the complex. Claire sensed the walls were advancing in on her, as the woods of Birnam had moved on Macbeth—threatening walls, that promised a horrible form of annihilation.

She simply couldn't drum up the compassion for the inmates she would have expected from herself. How could Nick endure the place—its omnipresent threshold of danger, the undercurrents of resentment, the whole edgy environment?

Under Henson's direction, the group moved on to a main dining room, a library, and classrooms, one equipped with computers. Although the general order when visitors roamed the halls kept inmates in their cells, a dozen worked at these computers behind locked doors. Claire noted that the two that did glance up and look at them through the thick-paned window had menacing, superior, most unwelcoming glances.

The last building on the agenda contained a power plant, boiler room and laundry. The prisoners here seemed to be conscientious older men employed in purposeful pursuits. Instead of the orange jumpsuits worn by the other inmates, these men had on slate-gray work shirts and pants.

Only one inmate was in the laundry, an unimpressive, overweight, and sullen individual of about fifty, his stomach bulging over his belt. He bore a resemblance to many stage-hands Claire had met on her tours—uncommunicative men generally, but up to their tasks and cooperative if you approached them without condescension.

Henson answered questions as they continued on. Claire paused a moment. Something had gotten into her eye. Standing behind the group, she rubbed her eyelid to generate tears to wash out the speck.

"Here's a clean towel you can use to get that out, lady," said the laundryman.

"Oh, thank you so much," she replied, "that's kind of you." She pulled up her eyelid and gently wiped across the cornea. "I think that did the trick." She started away quickly to catch up with her group, which was already exiting at the far end of the hall.

Suddenly she was yanked backward, down onto the stone floor. One massive hand dragged her by her arm into the laundry room, while the other clamped her mouth shut. She could neither scream nor bite the laundryman's massive hand.

The rough stone floor lacerated her hips and legs as he pulled her along. Her hips and legs burned with excruciating pain. The man hauled her into a storage room and pulled the door closed behind him. She let out a piercing scream as he threw her head down hard against the cement floor, stunning her into a semiconsciousness that made the room spin.

With beastlike groans, the man pushed a massive metal shelf against the door.

Her next scream was muffled by a piece of sheeting he tied brutally across her nose and mouth. Everything was done so quickly, Claire had no time to plan a strategy of resistance. The gag muffled all Claire's screams into choking whispers. It was so difficult to breathe; she couldn't think of anything else. To breathe became all-important.

The man stretched her arms up over her head, tying her wrists together with cord in a savage manner that tore the skin of her wrists, exposing nerve endings that pulsated with agony.

She tried to twist herself free, to bite away at the gag that was cutting viciously now on the right side of her jaw. With almost satanic glee, the man punched her across her face.

Oh, Lord Jesus, please come to my rescue. Forgive my indifference to You in the past. I beg You, help me. Carbon dioxide seemed to be about to explode her brain.

The man bent over her with eager, half-starved, craven eyes as he pressed his knees down hard against her hips and thighs. In lustful frenzy, he tore her skirt in two.

Death—her death at the hands of a madman—was imminent. Within moments, his crime would be discovered, and he'd face the severest of sentences. He must realize that. *God—oh, God, come quickly.*

What a fool she'd been—disregarding the basic rules—those simple rules Nick wanted her to be so mindful of. Here she was, seconds from death in this remote storeroom—only a few hundred yards from. . .

From approaching voices, accompanied by hurried stomping through the laundry. What seemed to be Nick's voice shouted above the rest, "Claire! Claire, can you hear me? We'll have you out of there in a minute."

The laundryman's mouth twisted in anger; his eyes bugged out with rage.

God had heard her. A miracle was on the other side of the door. Fiercely she tried to hold out against death, the carbon dioxide ballooning in her head, her chest falling in a desperate effort to exhale.

Above the hubbub beyond the door, she could hear Nick command Henson to take the students upstairs out of the area. A pounding like a battering ram forced the door open. Metal shelving clattered to the floor.

Nick was without his jacket, his short-sleeved shirt exposing the prostheses' cuffs attached on his lower arms. Prying the man's away from her with both prostheses, he hurled him against the wall. The man screamed in pain, throwing a fist at Nick, but Nick deflected the blow with the left prosthesis.

"Porter, nobody in this place swings at Van Vierssen," one of the guards intoned in a low, steady voice as he handcuffed the laundryman, ". . .because if he swings back—and don't for one minute think he won't—his hook could take an eye of yours with it."

The other guard dove to the floor to assist Nick in loosening Claire's gag. With the release of the first knot, she began to expel the carbon dioxide that had mushroomed in her head. She gulped the air. By the narrowest of margins she'd averted death. She was going to live. A prayer of thanksgiving filled her soul. *Thank You, Lord,* her brain kept repeating over and over—but her lips proved immobile.

"Do you want him in F-10?" asked the guard with the prisoner.

"That's best," Nick replied from his position on the floor. "I can manage here now, Drake," he said to the man who'd removed her gag.

"Are you sure?"

"Yes, I can handle everything with Ms. Rossiter. Just take care of Porter. Get him out of here. I'll be up later. And, thanks. I mean, this time we were winners. I appreciate it."

The guards pushed the prisoner ahead of them out of the room. Nick, his face glistening with perspiration, yanked away the remaining cord. His hook prosthesis scratched her, but she didn't mind.

He draped a sheet across her body. "Thank God, oh, thank God," he said in a barely audible moan. "You were on that tour with Henson only a few minutes before I realized I had to come down and be with you."

She wanted to tell him a million things—to apologize in some way for her reckless behavior. But her voice came in croaks and gasps. "Nick—I–I. . ." Her pummeled jaw and torn mouth had difficulty forming the words. "Sorry—"

"Claire, don't try to talk," he said. "Just relax, as best you can. I was out of my mind not to take you around myself right from the start."

Her jaw throbbed, her lips burned from the abrasive gag. "It was. . .all my. . .f–fault. My eye—he gave me. . .towel."

"Please don't talk, Claire. Your mouth is so badly bruised. Your cheeks are bleeding." He pressed a facecloth against her lips, then brushed her hair from her face. "I'll call the ambulance crew immediately. We have our own service in the prison, so it'll be only a few minutes and they'll have you on your way to the hospital in Fulton Falls."

"Nick, no. No hospital."

"Of course you'll go. It's important we get X-rays of your jaw and wrists, and get those wounds cleaned up. I want Doc Bremmer to check you over. It's mainly your face and hands, isn't it?" he asked, hesitantly, biting his upper lip. "Porter never managed to. . ."

"Rape me?" she whispered. "No."

He sighed, his relief obvious, as he tapped buttons on the telecommunication unit that hung from his belt. "Sam, Van

Vierssen here. We're going to have to have a stretcher in G-20. I'm with Ms. Rossiter now, in the laundry storage room. Phone the hospital and have Dr. Bremmer on duty in emergency. I'll stay here till the orderlies move her out. Yes, she looks good, all things considered. Oh, and Sam, send someone up to that professor. . .Jim Gleason in D-3. Tell him Claire is okay. Right. Just tell him she's going to be fine. Got that? Thanks."

He pressed off the unit. "Things'll be looking up soon, Claire."

"Sorry." She couldn't stop crying. "Didn't mean to disobey. I didn't tease—"

"Oh, honey, I know you didn't! You didn't do anything wrong!"

"He looked so innocent."

"Innocent? Oh, Claire, Porter was a professional hit man. Very innocent guy!" He raked the Greifer gently through her hair.

She shuddered with this disclosure. A hit man—no stranger to murder. "It was such a close call. Nick, I. . .I prayed."

"That makes two of us. God spared us a hideous 'might have been,' though this whole episode was bad enough."

"From the moment your group went through that sally port, I had misgivings. What madness to let you out of my sight in this place. I arrived at G-20 just as Henson started looking for you. The students tried to assure Henson and me that you were just back around the corner and everything would be okay, but Henson and I knew better. You 'free world' people have no idea what inmates are capable of."

He sat back against a concrete pillar, raised one knee and leaned his elbow on it. "Praise God, the guard came with equipment to ram through the door quickly."

He closed his eyes for a second. "I've seen some bad sights, Claire, and the nightmares that ran through my mind as we barreled into that door. . .well, all I can say is, I was actually relieved your situation wasn't worse."

He coughed nervously as his eyes sought hers again. "What a miracle to see you alive."

The poignancy of the moment was shattered by new voices in the laundry room. Two white-suited orderlies, carrying a stretcher, entered the storeroom. "Watch her wrists and jaw," Nick advised.

"Will do," said one of the attendants. "I'm sorry, miss; you're obviously hurtin' plenty," he said as he and the other attendant lifted her onto the stretcher. "We can't give you an injection for pain before Dr. Bremmer checks you over."

She was forced to grit her teeth to suppress a moan; the agony was so intense. They strapped a blanket over her.

"Claire, I can't ride to the hospital with you," said Nick, the crow's-feet around his eyes deepening, "because I'm not allowed to leave the compound until I get in a replacement. Also, I have to go up and have a little chat with that. . . ," he got to his feet and wiped his own forehead with a towel, ". . .with Porter. I'll have to write up a report. I may have to call his lawyer. We wouldn't want to deny Porter his legal rights, now, would we?"

He shook his head disgustedly as he went on, "But Doc Bremmer'll be at the hospital, Claire. He's a surgeon—top-notch—and a friend of mine. He'll take good care of you."

"Nick, I'm so, so sorry."

"Claire, things like this occur here almost every day. It's exceptional for me only because it happened to you, to an incredible and decent person like you. Please don't chastise yourself. You had a real problem, and Porter took advantage of it. Right now, we just have to get you comfortable and have you checked over. I'll get over to the hospital as soon as I can, and I'll have Jim stop to see you before he goes back to the campus."

"Nick, I. . ." She wanted so much to say "I love you," but the attendants were watching. She couldn't embarrass Nick in front of them.

They carried her out of the laundry room and down unpeopled corridors, doors electronically unlocking and locking behind them as they went along. Finally, they came to the entrance where the ambulance waited. No prisoners were around—just one guard, the two orderlies, and Nick.

The orderlies lifted her up into the ambulance. One of them climbed in with her. The other closed the door behind him. They then drove out of a gate and headed for the hospital, without the aid of sirens.

eleven

X-rays and a thorough examination by Dr. Bremmer showed mainly abrasions, cuts, and a seriously injured jaw and neck. "Tomorrow you'll be feeling better, but your face will be discolored. I regret having to tell you I'm holding off prescribing pain medication now because you may have suffered a mild concussion. We're going to keep you overnight for observation.

"Van Vierssen's coming in soon to check on you. Sister, you sure had him scared," he said, forming a teasing grin. "He's usually a cool cat about things up at that fun house of his. But this time, lady, he—well, he was majorly upset. He asked several times about your hands. You're a pianist, right?"

She managed a weak, "Yes."

"Your wrists are raw right now. But no great harm done. The ointment we put on should ease some of the sting. After head trauma like you've experienced, a patient often becomes drowsy even without heavy-duty pills or injections for pain. Don't be surprised if you fall asleep." Before he left her room, he and a nurse placed a foam collar around her neck to keep her head immobile. The collar and hand ointment, plus ice packs, gave her enough relief to doze off.

Later, she saw Jim standing by her bed, his face tense. She couldn't make out exactly what he said—something about the students driving her car back to the campus.

When she awoke, it was evening. Out of the corner of her eye, she could see Nick silhouetted by the sun, a few shocks of his hair reflecting the last rays of the day. He had changed into chino pants and a navy, wide-necked, short-sleeved yachting shirt—the prostheses' cuffs conspicuously attached to his arms. However, the hook prosthesis was gone, replaced by the synthetic hand on his left arm. His jacket lay across the adjustable table.

She spoke, calling to him in a faraway voice that required little movement of mouth and jaw. He hurried to her bed, and peered down at her with anxious eyes. "Welcome back to planet earth, darlin'." He shook his head and scowled. "I bet there isn't an inch of your body that doesn't hurt."

"Talking hurts. It hurts a lot, Nick—to talk."

"I'll do the talking for both of us. What good news, though. No broken bones and apparently no serious concussion."

Nick grinned now, the creases around his eyes crinkling in "up" fashion. "Don't worry about anything, Claire. Medical care here is all covered. And if you wish to press charges in the days ahead you'll certainly be. . ."

"I don't think I'll have any reason to do that."

"You might down the road. In any case, you'll have to write up a report for our files—but not today. Today you're going to concentrate on getting better and trying to erase trauma from your mind."

She nodded as much as pain or the collar would allow. "Nick, I prayed. In that storage closet, I did pray. And God answered my prayer. I'm relieved to be alive, and able to spend time here with you. Did you talk to Porter?"

He rubbed the back of the artificial hand along his chin. "Yes."

"He's a disturbed man, obviously. What will happen to him?"

"Wednesday he'll be shipped to another prison. With luck, he may end up in some rose-colored playground supervised by Arnie Saxby." He manipulated his Greifer several times seemingly to relieve tension as he continued, "Saxby can put him out to pasture. Just so long as he stays away from me. When something hits 'home' like this, Claire, a corrections officer can't be expected to work with that prisoner again. I'd assume it's like a doctor not delivering his own baby. Objectivity ceases."

Had she heard him right? Had he said, "hit home"? Was he talking about a husband-wife relationship? It sounded that way. Immobile as her neck was, her spirit was doing cartwheels. Her magnificent Nick of the courthouse, Nick of the plum-colored roses stood next to her, speaking to her as if she were his wife.

"Anyway," Nick went on, "it's in circumstances like this, Claire, where God's purposes seem so unclear. We keep asking why. When trauma's fresh, we have to hold onto faith that, in the big scheme of things, God does work for good with those He loves."

He blanketed her with a tender glance. "Claire, we turn to the story of Job. Where were any of us, when God created the behemoth? So how can we grasp the way we fit into His scheme of things?"

How can we indeed? Claire asked herself. She wasn't noticing Greifers anymore. Nick's fathomless eyes, his strong face, his caring smile so dominated his person that prostheses faded into the background.

"Try not to be too upset, Nick," she managed, though her mouth moved painfully as she spoke the words, "I don't need behemoths. Being with you is proof enough that God's out there, planning good things for me. Dr. Bremmer says I'll be fine by the end of the week. Since I have no recitals pending, perhaps I can take the time to compose more jazz variations."

"Hey, that's the way to go," he replied with enthusiasm. "Or, why don't you take a stab at a musical? Since you love France, set the scene in the French Revolution. Turn out something on Dickens's *A Tale of Two Cities*—Madame De Farge knitting at the guillotine. She'd be a contralto, I think, don't you?"

"Absolutely."

"Or you could tackle *The Three Musketeers*. Something Debussyish for Porthos would be catchy."

She could hardly control a belly laugh at this absurd suggestion. Debussy's wistful melodies could never set the scene for the burly Porthos. "Please don't kid around like that, Nick. Laughing smarts!"

"I'm sorry. But I'm only half joking. You could manage an operetta or a musical comedy, no trouble at all."

His prostheses rested on the bed rail, and he leaned down over her, his face so temptingly close that she craved his lips. Ironically, she was now the handicapped one. Her arms and her hands were the limbs that lay helpless, too weak to bring his head to hers. On impulse, she found herself saying, "Nick, I'm not so bruised that I wouldn't welcome a kiss."

"Claire, I can't do that—your cheeks and mouth are much too sore for. . ."

"Just a fifty-cent kiss—on my forehead."

He did nothing for a few seconds. Then he lowered the bed railing and brought his face to hers. Putting his right arm carefully under her head, he kissed her first in feather-duster fashion on her lips, then more firmly on her cheek and more firmly still on her forehead.

Slowly he pulled away from her, and she looked up at him. "We simply must never lose each other again," she whispered.

His mouth had formed an ethereal smile, the type one might receive from a cloistered Trappist monk on the other side of a monastery gate. *Yet,* she tried to tell herself, *no gates could ever come between us after the experience of this day.*

A nurse barged into the room. "Excuse me, but it's 8:30— time for visitors to depart. Oh, wait a minute, Dr. Bremmer has given you permission, Mr. Van Vierssen, to stay through the night with this patient, hasn't he?"

Nick nodded. "Yes, he has."

Claire looked up in surprise. "Is that correct? You're staying throughout the whole night, Nick?"

"Um-hum, yes, the whole night." He went over to the nurse. "Our patient hasn't had anything since breakfast. I think she could go for some liquid refreshment besides water."

The nurse looked at her chart once again. "Dr. Bremmer

wants her to lay low on intake because of the possible concussion."

"I realize that," Nick replied, "but couldn't she have a small juice or soda?"

The woman smiled. "I'm sure we can get something to tide her over."

Once the nurse had left the room, Claire spoke out in a startled voice. "Nick, how can you plan to stay here all night when you need your rest to cope with the governor's reception tomorrow?"

"Claire, I've slept in enough uncomfortable positions in my life to know I'll get sufficient rest in that chair by the window. . .for the governor or anyone who happens by. Even wild horses ridden by the governor won't deter me from my vigil here with you tonight. If I hadn't been so neglectful of you earlier today, the ordeal with Porter would never have happened."

"Actually," she said somewhat sheepishly, "I'm awfully glad you're going to be here. I'm feeling a bit trembly, I admit."

"I'm sure you are."

"But I'm not sleepy."

"I'll sit beside you and keep you entertained."

Nick was well into reminiscing about an experience he'd had at a church camp when he was interrupted by the nurse's arrival with two milk shakes. "One's for you, Mr. Van Vierssen," she announced with a big grin. "Dr. Bremmer thought you needed a treat yourself."

Nick laughed as he got up to assist the nurse in arranging the bed and table so Claire could drink from the straw.

"Dr. Bremmer also phoned the desk just to check on you. Because you're signed in for the night, you're not to leave the hospital until 3:00 tomorrow. Dr. Bremmer also added an emphatic message for you, Mr. Van Vierssen: If you spend the night here, you're to behave yourself as a gentleman, under the staff's strictest supervision."

Nick shook his head as he winked at Claire and took a sip of his milk shake. "Tell Doc Bremmer I'm promising nothing."

"I'll convey your message," the nurse giggled as she headed for the door. "If the milk shake doesn't give you grief, Ms. Rossiter, I'll return with ibuprofen in an hour."

"I bet you're glad to get that news, Claire," Nick said. "At ten o'clock I'm going to tuck you in and insist we both call it a day and try to get some sleep."

ò

Claire woke up with the sun sending shafts of light across the floor. To her dismay, when she called to Nick, he didn't answer. He wasn't there. Her dismay, however, was short-lived. Nick, with a trace of light-colored whiskers, bustled into the room with the morning nurse who carried a breakfast tray—only soft cream cereal, orange juice, and coffee, but a breakfast, nevertheless.

"Do you think you can manage breakfast okay by yourself, Claire?" Nick asked after the nurse had gone.

"Yes." *As little of it as I'll take. My neck and head hurt more today than yesterday—but I'm not about to tell him that.*

"I'm going to have to leave in a few minutes," Nick reminded her. "There's the governor, as you know, who's probably assembling his white-gloved troops for the afternoon inspection of my august institution."

"May I suggest you shave before you meet the governor," she offered as she took a sip of coffee.

"Do you really think I have to?" He scowled petulantly.

"I do, yes," she said with mock severity.

"All right. I'll take care of that to please you and the governor. There are a few logistical details I have to sort out with you before we head back to your campus this evening. You'll need to have something to wear. Tell me your dress size so I can go into Ridglea later this morning to get you a suitable exit ensemble."

"But, Nick, is that really necessary?"

"I insist, sweet maiden." He looked quickly at his watch.

"Okay, since I have to add shaving to my agenda, I better get going. Quick now, tell me the size I should ask for at the dress shop in Ridglea."

"I can't let you do this for me, Nick, I. . ."

"And how, in your condition, are you going to stop me? Behave yourself and tell me your size."

"You've got to let me reimburse you."

His mouth pursed in disgust, as he took an exasperated deep breath. "Woman, how do I tolerate this nonsense of yours? If you don't tell me your size, I'll ask the nurses—or I'll guess. And if I do that, you may end up with an atrocious tent. It'll be your own fault."

She snickered as she replied, "I wear size eight tall."

"Eight tall it is."

"You are, without a doubt, the most impossibly forceful, dear, and outrageous tyrant I've ever run across."

"That's my job description, honey." He leaned down over her breakfast tray, wiped her chin with a napkin, and gave her a good-bye kiss. "The nurses tell me they'll have you ready to depart the premises at 6:00. I'll see that the store delivers your new outfit in plenty of time for you to get yourself into it for your journey."

❧

By noon, Claire realized the throbbing in her jaw and neck had abated considerably. No question, the ibuprofen helped a great deal. After assisting her with a shower, an aide put her in a clean gown and robe, affixed the foam collar around her neck, and told her she was free to walk about the hospital.

Looking at herself in the bathroom mirror, Claire was horrified. Her face was swollen and grotesque. Dark blue-black discoloration permeated her entire left cheek, down through her neck. Her left eye was bloodshot. A large area of her lips was scabbing up. "I'm a monster!"

However, walking about the pleasant little hospital facility buoyed her spirits. From a sunroom she looked out onto a garden where a few purple-veined crocuses strained their heads to speak to the sun.

No one would ever guess that a few miles over the hills in the distance Everettsville prison covered a barren valley. It would be a nice day for the governor's reception. She could picture Nick greeting the contingent from the capital. He'd be dressed in an exceedingly well-tailored suit, maybe the one he'd worn to her recital. Like everyone else, the governor would be impressed by him. Then, if the pattern held true, he'd be uncomfortable noticing Nick's disability. . .but with lighthearted remarks, Nick would put him at ease, and the moment would be quickly behind them.

Nick's handicap wasn't something that had a long-term effect on people's relationships with him. Claire was convinced it would no longer be a factor in the relationship she had with him, either.

At 1:00, Nick's package arrived from the dress shop. Folded carefully in layers of tissue paper were chic delphinium blue slacks, an exquisite silk blouse of the same shade, along with a matching faux-suede jacket. Without a doubt, it was one of the loveliest ensembles Claire had ever seen. At the bottom of the box, in a discreet bag, lay packaged undergarments next to a blue voile scarf. In the folds of the scarf was a typed note. "For the veiled look, in case you're sensitive about your rainbow-hued face en route. Nick."

She grinned as she read this. Yes, it would indeed be a good idea to have a scarf handy to tie loosely around her face, especially if they stopped anywhere and got out of the car.

twelve

It was well past six before Nick got to the hospital. Claire sat in the hospital foyer, dressed in her new outfit. An aide had attractively fixed her hair.

He helped her up. "That outfit's ideal for you," he exclaimed, delight evident on his face. "I'll have to admit, it's the perfect shade for you under the present circumstance because there's no doubt about it; your face really is blue, Cindy Sue."

"You're mean," she snapped. "Generous to a fault, a man of exceptionally good taste, and very irresistible—but still mean."

Fortunately, the pain in her mouth and jaw had abated sufficiently for her to put her arms around his waist and give him a tiny hug.

He whispered in her ear, "Actually, honey, you look one hundred percent better today. With your hair curled forward like that, most of the bruised area's covered." He backed away slowly and looked her up and down. "You're a stunning woman, Claire, bluebird jaw and all. I'm glad you've shed the foam collar, but you may want to use it in the car."

"I'll try going without it for a while."

"Be sure to have it handy, just in case."

She picked up a plastic bag from the floor. "It's right here."

Claire could almost feel all the eyes in the foyer gazing at them. Gossip being what it is, she suspected everyone knew about her monstrous ordeal at the prison.

Virtually everyone in the hospital knew Nick, who at that moment was a splendid sight to behold. No question about it—he had come directly from the dinner for the governor. Although he wasn't wearing the sophisticated pinstripe he'd worn at her concert, the suit he was wearing was a standout. . . steel gray with a subtle sheen, radiating power, class, and

114

authority. Above suit and tie, Claire noticed, was his normally closely shaven face—the face she dearly loved.

He took the bag from her and led her out to his car, an understated late-model silver sports coupe with sunroof. Claire wasn't prepared, however, for custom-made pressure-panels on doors so Nick could open them. Nor was she ready for knobs on the steering wheel.

Sadly, she had to admit to herself, she'd failed to conquer all the queasiness about his handicap over the last few monu-mentally transforming hours. Out here in the big, wide world were circumstances she hadn't bargained for—cars, for exam-ple, that had adjustments so Nick could cope.

He was wearing both Greifers—because, she supposed, he needed as much dexterity as possible, driving the highway and caring for her.

Once satisfied she was comfortable, he went around and got into his side of the car. They were soon on the highway, wind-ing into hills north of town with which Nick obviously had great familiarity. It was a warm evening, warm enough to keep the sunroof slightly open. As they headed onto the thruway and increased their speed, the breeze carried with it the fragrance of newly-turned earth and awakened wildflowers.

Nick turned on a CD. "If you'd rather listen to Beethoven," he commented after a minute or two of light rock, "I think the Eighth Symphony's in that case there."

"No, the CD that's playing is pleasant. I don't often relax listening to Beethoven because I'm always analyzing it—anticipating the orchestral techniques in the development."

He laughed. "I'm that way watching prison shows on TV. Always studying the procedures portrayed. When you know too much about a subject, the errors in script or performance bombard you. You can't take your shoes off, sit back, and just enjoy it."

"I'd like to see you with your shoes off—just relaxing some evening, watching TV."

She noticed him inhale deeply between tightened lips.

She'd accidentally stumbled on a subject—whatever it might be—that upset him.

"What I mean is," she explained, trying to extricate herself, "you're nearly always dressed up—ready to give a speech, or coming from a governor's reception. Like tonight, for example, even though you don't have a tie on, you look sensational in that tweed jacket. I hope you don't think you have to dress up all the time with me, Nick. As it turns out, I've hardly ever seen you without a jacket—in casual attire, like on Saturday afternoon."

"And was it shocking to you?" he replied much too seriously.

"You mean because. . ."

"Because you could see where the prostheses join my arms?"

"No, because I'd seen that before. At Jim's party."

"Claire," he said with a determination she found unsettling, "relaxing for me often means taking off one or both of my prostheses. That kind of relaxation you wouldn't want to see."

"Silly. I can't imagine not wanting to see you any way at all, with or without your prostheses."

Staring straight ahead, he spoke in barely audible tones, "When I'm alone in my room with all this equipment off—nobody sees me like that."

A chill came over her. She touched his arm, soothingly. "Nick, I'm sorry I've upset you. Let's change the subject. Have you talked with Jim since he's been back?"

He continued to look out over the wheel, but followed her suggestion to direct the conversation elsewhere. "Yes, I phoned him earlier today. I told him I was driving you back home and that you'd need a student to give you some assistance for a few days. I know Peg can't be of much help because she's so busy with the baby. But surely someone can get over to help you out."

"Oh, I can always call Irene Dabrovsky. I'm feeling so much better, Nick, that—"

"Be *sure* to call Irene, Claire—or someone. You aren't supposed to get those wrists wet. And I know you'll be on the pain medication for a few more days. Jim said he had called your department. They're assigning a grad student to teach your lessons."

"I'm glad that's taken care of."

"Jim and Peg wanted us to stop for dinner tonight, but I told them we'd eat on the way. There's an Italian restaurant up the road. Maybe you could manage a sip or two of minestrone—or possibly some manicotti."

He turned his head for a second and tossed her the hint of a smile.

"I'll give manicotti a try," she replied.

They drove on in silence for a while, Nick seeming to concentrate on thoughts he didn't wish to share with her.

"Did Jim say the students enjoyed their outing at the prison?" she asked, tongue in cheek, breaking the silence.

"We sure gave them something to write home about, didn't we?" She was relieved to see a bit of merriment had returned to his face. "I hope we scared some of those girls out of a career in penology—at least in an institution like Everettsville."

"With proper training they might prove themselves valuable in time, Nick."

"I suppose. I'm still disturbed by women personnel in a male institution. And it's even getting legally tougher and tougher to make any judgment calls about where we place them."

What was on his mind? She was certain there was more to this conversation than was evident on the surface. "*Some* of the women must be effective in these jobs, though," she offered.

"Yes, some. A few spiritual souls who dress in a subdued fashion and aren't so well-endowed by nature that they immediately direct the men's attention to those endowments. But take yourself, Claire. How could you ever look unattractive enough to divert a man's attention from *your* alluring womanhood? It couldn't be done.

"By way of example, a year ago an attractive young woman

came in to teach ceramics. A jealous inmate put a contract out on her husband, hiring an accomplice on the outside to murder him on his way to work. His altruistic-but-naive wife had a breakdown that required hospitalization."

Claire shuddered. The men in the Fulton Falls courthouse had discussed contracts on Nick himself.

Hesitantly she asked, "Nick, have there been—I mean, have you had any contracts put out on you?"

"A few. Quite a while ago, actually."

"And that doesn't terrify you? What I'm trying to say. . ."

"At first, it did. But the Lord has brought me through so many skirmishes, like the one we both faced with Porter, that I have to turn to Psalm 18 and believe He rescues me from violent enemies. Also, I'm convinced that it helps to be an amputee."

The darkness of Nick's mood was intensified by the blackness of the interstate as the car plunged through the night.

"What are you trying to tell me, Nick?"

"Merely that I think the inmates don't look upon me as someone to envy."

Nick's honest evaluation of his circumstances bombarded her senses once again. Few people *would* envy him. Arnold Saxby had told her *he* didn't.

The governor probably hadn't either.

As the road veered off to the right, she noticed a lighted exit sign over the highway in the distance, backed by the neon lights of a rest stop. Nick took that exit.

"I'm sure they feel I've already had a contract done on me," Nick continued, "and that hasn't made me grovel. A future contract, short of death, wouldn't do the job for them anyway. The restaurant's just ahead; it's a good one, with high, dark booths that conceal hooks and jaws and anything that might happen to give you embarrassment."

The small-town diner was crowded and poorly lighted. Nick directed her to a corner booth.

"What can I get you, warden?" asked the waitress, who recognized Nick.

Claire wondered what the woman thought, seeing Nick, a prison official, escorting a woman with a highly battered face.

Not so battered, fortunately, that she couldn't eat manicotti.

At first, it upset her to notice the difficulty Nick had with his utensils. But because he didn't seem unduly embarrassed, after a few moments, she was able to overlook his awkwardness enough to enjoy her meal.

The main thrust of the conversation was Nick's insistence she direct her talents into composing a musical. Such a project wasn't pie-in-the-sky fantasy, as far as he was concerned.

"Claire, you should focus on a project like that over the next few months, till your wrists heal," Nick said with fervor. "Forget everything else."

It jarred her a bit the way he stressed "everything else" with that faraway look in his blue eyes.

"It's something to think about," she answered, knowing full well that both of them were skirting the subject that filled their minds—namely, their personal lives and their destiny together, if any.

Once they were back in the car, Nick continued to avoid these issues by talking about prisoners he'd dealt with over the years.

"But, Nick, how on earth did you ever get into corrections in the first place?" she asked.

"My career choice was made when, in a rehab hospital, I became friends with a kid of about thirteen named Rick, who was crippled in both legs—and blind. It seems Rick's uncle appeared from out of the blue and had sent Rick into the streets to peddle drugs. The poor kid misplaced a package of heroin, and his uncle became enraged. He pummeled the youngster with fists and crowbar, crippling and blinding Rick for life."

Claire cringed. "A monster, a madman something like, er— like Porter?"

Taking a deep breath, Nick spoke in a voice both deliberate and soft. "Not exactly. A shade worse, I'd say, because this man was deranged by drugs. But, like Porter, he was a convicted murderer. He had escaped from a penitentiary, so you could say a careless prison staff was responsible for Rick's misery. When I learned this, I was so livid I wanted to phone the White House, or the FBI, or *someone* on the boy's behalf.

"I didn't, of course. At the time I could barely use a telephone. But I started reading everything I could on the subject of penology, convinced that this was to be my ministry. In time, I enrolled in a university program in corrections in California. It's been my commitment ever since, Claire, to spare a few other kids a fate like Rick's."

"I bet your family was less than overjoyed about your career choice. Ten to one they tried to get you to change your mind."

He rubbed his chin as he nodded. "Ah, yes. They made every effort to talk me out of penology. My dad even tried to convince me I'd never be hired because I wouldn't be able to fire a gun. But I fooled him and rigged up a pistol I could handle. Then I badgered some people in high places to give me a chance. My dad was a vice admiral in the navy before he retired, so he has a few friends who pull weight in Washington. That didn't hurt my chances. But what it basically came down to is, there was a shortage of personnel in a facility near Hartford, so I got the job."

Hartford—she'd performed in Hartford once. Playing her concert there, she'd given nary a thought to prisons.

"So that goes to show you, Claire," he declared, "that once the Lord taps you on the shoulder for something, He also gives you the persistence and the imagination—and the opportunities—to follow through with it. But you're right; it didn't thrill my folks. They'd have preferred my going into my dad's business."

Curious, Claire commented, "I gather that resembles in no way, shape, or form, a penitentiary."

He chuckled. "Not hardly. He runs a marina and mast and rigging outfit down near Norfolk. For centuries, the Van

Vierssens have been men who went out to sea in ships."

"Operating sailboats on the Chesapeake sounds sensational to me. How could you refuse such a—"

"Oh, Claire, that would be the worst place for me. When I'm down there I can take a motorboat out for a spin. That's done simply by turning a key. But working with masts and ropes would be out of the question for someone with my disability. In my dad's company, I'd be no more than an overprotected office drone."

They'd arrived at the campus, and he was driving around the parade grounds to Regent Street. "When all is said and done, I've found an important job in which I excel. I've found my own little corner of the universe where I can perform a service.

"Also," he said, enunciating each word much too carefully, "I'm in a field where being single is a distinct advantage. So that's important, too."

"But, Nick," she choked out after a split second of shocked silence, "you don't expect to be single all your life. Not anymore. Not after. . ."

He stared intently at the street ahead and moistened his lips several times before he spoke.

"I'm never going to get married, Claire; marriage can't be a part of my world. It's something a guy like me couldn't cope with. I'm sorry, but I just couldn't share my private pain with a woman I loved."

She was aghast by the finality with which he said these words—so stupefied, she couldn't answer him.

He pulled into her driveway behind her hatchback, which had been parked there by the students Saturday night. Switching off the engine, he turned to her.

"Claire, you're not well enough to discuss anything heavy tonight. It's unfortunate that the subject of marriage came up. But, since it did, I must convey to you right now the realities of my life, and why marriage is out for me."

She grasped his arm. "Nick, you can't possibly mean that

after all we've been through this weekend, there's no future for us—none at all."

"You've got to be brave for both of us," he appealed. "Let me help you out of the car. I'll fix you some tea, coffee, cocoa, whatever, and make you comfortable so you can get some sleep."

He was leaning away, sliding out of the car. "We'll talk it over inside," he said. He went around and opened her door. "Come on, now, up you go. You'll understand better after I've explained things to you."

"I'll never understand," she stammered as she stepped out of the car. He pulled her toward him, his face a breath away from hers.

"My darling Claire, sometimes we have to face up to tragedy head-on, with squared shoulders and no emotion whatsoever. The Lord *does* expect this now and then. Isaiah tells us that the direction we might like to go isn't necessarily the way the Lord would want us to go. He often has a higher way. Frequently, it's tough for us to accept that higher way. Years ago I had to face up to this handicap of mine. Tonight I'm going to have to help you face up to it, too."

"Nick, I *have* faced up to it," she cried, allowing her shoulder to fall under his muscular arm, as he walked her to the door. "I've come such a long way these past few months. Seeing you with a serious disability saddens me, yes. I think it's dreadful, but our not being together would be more dreadful. I can't bear the thought of that anymore."

"Let's have your key so we can go inside," he stated. "We can't stand out here indefinitely. You need to lie down."

She fumbled in her purse for the key. Shaking, she inserted it into the lock.

With both prostheses, plus her weak assistance, Nick pushed open the door.

thirteen

Once inside, Claire clutched Nick's arms tightly, despite throbbing pain coursing through her arms and jaw, making her eyes water.

"Nick, I will not accept this. You're indispensable in my life now. I'm sure you care for me as well. That's what's destroying me—knowing that you care for me but won't admit it. Jesus personifies compassion and gentle kindness. He couldn't possibly expect us to go our separate ways."

Nick took a deep breath but said nothing, letting her continue. "I'm not as familiar with Scripture passages as you are, but I've felt from the moment I first met you that there was more than coincidence in all of this. It was a manifestation of divine direction. We *have* to see each other again—and often—if for no other reason than that we are God-anointed best friends. You have become"—she pulled away and glanced up at him—"my dearest friend."

He shook his head several times. "Claire, I *can't* see you again. We're already well beyond friendship. We've reached a point of agony. Certainly I have. Going on like this will bring me to marriage or madness, or should I say marriage *and* madness. Marriage is out of the question because insanity is something I *know* the Lord doesn't want."

"Nick, why is marriage so out of the question? I have no intention of wrenching you away from your ministry to prisoners. Couldn't we, as married people, come up with some satisfactory arrangement? If you worried about my safety near the prison, I could continue living here—keeping my own name—and we could be together on weekends. Or I could live in the city. It's only a short sprint from Everettsville. We'd have an unlisted phone number. . . ."

123

"Claire, stop all this nonsense."

With needlelike pain racing down her arms, she had to let go of him. Her legs could barely hold her up.

Nick caught her to prevent her from falling. Steadying her with his strong right arm, he helped her to the sofa in the living room.

He knelt down next to her on one knee. "You're exhausted, Claire. Why, oh, *why* must we torture ourselves talking about marriage when it can never happen for us?"

Frantic pleading poured from her lips. "For me, it's got to happen. God respects the kind of love I have for you, Nick. How can you toss me aside? You love me! Don't try to tell me otherwise. I *know* you do."

"That's not the major thing to consider. . . ."

"It is for me. Frankly, I'd just like to hear you tell me, yes or no: Are you in love with me?"

Nick put an elbow on the edge of the couch and allowed his head to fall down on the hand prosthesis. His voice was barely audible. "Claire, of course I'm in love with you. A man would have to be blind, deaf, and demented not to love you. I'm so crazy about you, I can't even keep my thoughts straight anymore."

"So, if you love me, what kind of gamble is there?" She sat up and wove her fingers through a strand of his exquisite hair. "We can go on much as we've been doing in our careers. We have incomes satisfactory to keep us solvent. We're both Christians, and I'd so enjoy your teaching me more about God. Nick, I understand and accept your handicap completely, and. . ."

Extricating himself away from her touch, he stood up and moved away from her, then abruptly turned back. "Claire, that's precisely the problem. You do *not* understand my handicap completely. You could never accept it." His beautiful lips enunciated these words softly but with a terrifying insistence.

"What absurdity! I hardly think about your prostheses or your limitations anymore," she replied, her voice, as well as her entire body, trembling out of control. "I was attracted to you before I knew you had any handicap. I've accepted the fact that you have one. I could manage as your wife very well."

He walked slowly over to the fireplace. Putting both his arms down on the mantel, he rested his head on his arms for several minutes. Then he raised it slowly.

"So you think you know me, Claire," he said, his face now addressing the bricks of the chimney. "Would it surprise you to know that at this moment I'm a most unrighteous individual? I'm identifying with Porter—Porter, that murderous goon who nearly killed you in the storage room. And you know what? I'm as miserable a slob as he is. I desperately, frantically want to make love to you. Right now, I'm envious of that punk."

He attempted a halfhearted, almost sardonic smile. "I'm jealous of him and all the other Porters of the world who have the capacity to touch you—to finger your beautiful face and caress your body."

He pounded one of his prostheses down on the mantel with a violent thud. "I'm so torn up inside with desire for you that *I'm* close to the brink myself."

She wanted to scream her outrage. But the screams caught in her throat, a throat paralyzed in incredulity, causing those screams to emerge as gasps.

"I'm every bit as big a ghoul as the Porters of that hole of a prison, Claire," Nick continued. "The only difference is that I'm locked in a different kind of prison—with a life sentence and no key—so even if I wear a three-hundred-dollar suit, speak more coherently than Porter, and beg God to forgive me, I'm no better than he is. I want you the same way he did—maybe more."

"Nick," she finally hurled back at him, "what you're saying is outrageous. You're nothing like Porter."

Tears surged from her eyes. She hurried to him and leaned full against his back, her face now pulsing with pain against the arch of his spine. "How could you think such hideous thoughts? Is it wrong to admit that you're a human being? Did God create you to be an emotionless automaton? So you have machine fingers; does that mean you're to replace a sensitive and loving spirit with some sort of machine there, as well?"

Her words stumbled forth between sobs. "Loving me is not a mortal sin, Nick. It's natural. It's wonderful. I *want* you to desire me. And I want to return your love. Furthermore, I'm confident we can make it. Why don't you at least let us give it a try?"

"No! We can't, Claire. We can't!" he shouted. It frightened her to hear him shout. "That's exactly what we cannot do—give it a try."

He turned to her, his lips tight, obviously attempting to keep his emotions in check. In a more controlled voice he went on. "That's the reason it won't work, don't you see, darling? Because it would be an experiment, an experiment filled with appalling embarrassment and frustration for us both. In a lab, if an experiment fails, the scientist starts over again with clean vials, discarding the original contents. And *you* could do that! You could go back to your millionaire backers and your friends on campus, chalking up our marriage as an experiment that just didn't happen to work out. Isn't that true?"

For a second or two she was tongue-tied by the savage scrutiny of his eyes. It was not an idle accusation he was making. He really believed there was truth in those odious words.

"I resent that," she seethed. "It would not be just an experiment. Granted, I've been a lapsed Christian, but I would not take the vows of matrimony lightly. I'd never think of marriage to you as a mere experiment."

"It would have to be, Claire, because there are so many things you don't know about, and probably couldn't live with. What I'm trying to say is that *you* could survive a divorce or an annulment. But I couldn't."

His voice had become distant and introspective. "I think you should be sitting down. You aren't strong enough to stand for so long."

He put an arm around her waist and propelled her back to the sofa. "I want you to lie still and let me try to explain as honestly and candidly as I can the complications of this situation."

The weight of disillusionment more than the pain in her face caused her to slump onto the sofa. Her jaw throbbed unmercifully as she lowered it against a pillow he had positioned there.

"Why don't you let me get you a cup of tea?" he asked.

She shook her head.

"Coffee?"

"Nothing."

He slid to the floor and sat catty-corner to her, his back against the side unit of the sofa, one of his knees raised. He looked up at her and continued. "Claire, you may think I'm being exceedingly selfish about all this, that I'm not thinking about you. Trust me when I say that I am. Some of my friends in various hospitals were married—several of them fathers of young children. I saw whole families dissolve over handicaps like mine—in most cases, they weren't even as debilitating as mine. I saw men of brilliant mind and supreme courage crumple into madness. In fact, I'm one of the fortunate ones. Do you believe that? It's true; I am.

"I often think the fact that I'd been at the Naval Academy was the main reason I made it. That sounds ridiculous in light of the fact that if I hadn't gone to Annapolis the accident wouldn't have happened at all. Ironically, though, the training I had there made the difference in my recovery."

He stretched his arms up behind him along the edge of the cushions. "You see, I had to stand in formation and put up with little annoyances like a mosquito on my forehead—or an unbearable itch on my arm. That discipline, being able to endure tactile irritation without flinching, got me through the early weeks after the accident. Navy discipline, superb help from my parents, chaplain Buck Wilson with a faith that moved mountains, and a terrific hospital staff kept me on keel. So I'm in pretty good shape, all things considered."

"Nick, I think you'd have come through successfully no matter where you went to school or who was at your bedside," she stammered. "You're the most mature human being I've ever met."

"Oh, darling Claire, you can't imagine what it's been like. I haven't always been mature. Oh, man," he groaned, "many days I—I—well, I can only say I was anything but mature."

Inhaling deeply, he leaned his head back against the sofa seat and stared at the ceiling. "You can't begin to comprehend my limitations—just from what you've observed when we've been together. Even in that laundry room, when you saw I couldn't untie the gag quickly enough and had to let Drake do it, that's just the tip of the iceberg. Beneath this facade of conventional exterior, Claire, is the most barbarous of creatures. If you could see me in the privacy of my shower—after I've removed these plastic cuffs, fixtures, and batteries—if you could witness the helplessness of your beloved, you'd be wretched and overcome with revulsion."

"Stop it!" she stormed at him, rising to reach down and press her hand firmly on his knee. "I won't let you go on castigating yourself like that. It's fruitless and it takes us nowhere."

"Hear me out, Claire, just hear me out, because you won't understand fully unless I tell you these things. You could never fathom how helpless I am."

Galuppi had come in and jumped up on Nick's lap. Looking down at the cat, Nick began stroking him slowly. "I'm what is known in medical circles as a wrist and below-elbow bilateral amputee," he continued. "That's basically what I amount to in clinical terms. And you should know those terms.

"Because I was a decent enough athlete as a youngster, I have well-developed muscles that respond favorably to state-of-the-art devices that can perform a motion that brings two or three surfaces in opposition, allowing for grasp of objects. Easy? Automatic? No, it's difficult in the extreme, requiring effort and great concentration that I often wish I could ignore once in a while.

"I was lucky to have had superlative surgery, but besides the normal phantom pain, which can be excruciating, I have an unusual problem: sensitive skin. My stumps often become tingly. I get severe prickly aggravation, even swelling. On hot days, I can develop irritation, itching, and occasionally a rash—a bit like you might, if you were to wear plastic gloves night and day. When that happens, I desperately look forward to the hour when I can return to my quarters, remove one or both of these prostheses, and finally put my stumps on a horizontal surface—preferably my bed—and cool off."

She stared down at him, feeling ill. Why was he talking about such things as "stumps," a term so gross that hearing it prompted waves of nausea to well up in her stomach?

He went on. "I have a wand that I can manipulate with my teeth—or my stumps together, if I want to turn pages of a book, or turn on the television, or make a phone call. A pencil with an eraser can be effective also. I can put the wand or pencil in the crook of my elbow and function somewhat.

"But neither of these things can open doors, so I live in constant dread of fire. Even with my prostheses *on* I'm in mortal fear of fire. Occasionally I have nightmares about it. I pray the Lord will one day release me from this fear, but He hasn't yet. I never close my door or window tightly, if I can help it."

Trembling with this revelation, Claire realized she had *not* envisioned these horrors. Suppressed sobs escaped her chest.

But Nick's modulated voice drove onward. "An amputee learns over many months that if he's going to make it, he has to start compensating for the loss of his hands with toes, teeth, chin—you name it. I'm sure it will come as a surprise to you to learn that I'm remarkably dexterous with my toes. The truth is, I can sign my name with my toes as well as I can with my Greifer. Most people are revolted by this accomplishment, so I don't mention it often."

He paused. Gradually his head turned to her. He sighed in despair before proceeding. "Perhaps you have some curiosity as to how I get dressed or put on these mechanical hands. It's truly a sight to behold. My gyrations and contortions with arms, knees, and chin are not a pretty sight. My mother saw me getting into my paraphernalia once, Claire, and fainted; a rescue squad had to come to the house. How do you think it feels to see someone I love collapse at the sight of me getting ready for my day's occupation?"

His eyes pierced hers. However, there was no sign of anger present in eyes or in tone of voice, just an eerie persistence.

"There are even more unsavory situations that I won't go into, but I think you get the drift. How long after a wedding do you think you could endure witnessing my existence? A week? A month, maybe? Perhaps a year, with God's help. But that would be pushing it, don't you suppose?

"And, as I said before, once we split up, you could make a promising future for yourself—you know you could. You could return to Henri in Paris, and he'd welcome you with open arms—open arms ending in fingers of flesh. But what would that do to me? My psychological survival would be at stake."

Ignorant of the tension of the moment, Galuppi slept, purring on Nick's lap. "St. Paul tells us, Claire, in his first letter to the Corinthians, that love doesn't insist on its own way. Any love we have for each other cannot insist on *its* own way. The prison community depends on me. God depends on me to do His work there. Furthermore, I can't present to my father and mother in their senior years a son who is mad as well as mutilated. Marriage is not in the Lord's plan for me, despite your thoughts to the contrary. To become involved with you is to destroy myself."

He raised his arm and rested it gently on her legs. "Tell me, how could I let you go if you were my wife? If I had kissed you as passionately, albeit clumsily, as I desire to, and we had consummated our love? How could I face your looks of pity, the moisture welling in your eyes day in and day out? Or the clenched teeth as you went about 'seeing things through.' It's tough enough to see my parents responding this way when I visit them. But every day, with you as my wife. . .well, it would be impossible. And when you finally decided you had to leave, I could *not* survive it. It will be hard enough to survive *today*—or this week."

He pressed a prosthesis against one eye for a few seconds, then let it slam down to the floor by his side. Claire's whole body shook, and she felt tears spilling from her eyes.

"Claire, Porter's savage attack on you all but did me in emotionally. Yes, it's going to be no small task to recover from this week. My existence up to now has been plodding along, better than I ever expected it would. I contribute significantly in my field. The Lord has worked through me to salvage many lives. Like St. Paul, with his thorn in the flesh, I witness victories. Can any of us hope for much more than that, in Christ's name? I don't think we can."

"Nick, I. . . ," she began, but found she was unable to formulate any sensible reply. Her lips were limp. Nick's words had left her spirit limp, as well.

"Look at yourself," he said with the hint of a smile, in an attempt at cheerfulness. "The mishap that befell you won't affect your performances in the long run. You'll have recitals galore. What's more, you're going to turn your attention to composing, allowing the Holy Spirit to inspire you to write music that may well edify thousands."

But she was unable to think of herself or her future. The sting of his statements about his tragic existence had seared her brain, prompting reevaluation. She had wormed her way into the life of a noble human being whose private world was a living nightmare.

She had tempted him most sinfully. The fact that she'd pushed him, a man she idolized, to this unhappy point made her feel cheap, almost sadistic, and full of remorse.

If she really loved him—and she did, in a way she never could have believed possible to love any man—she would have to allow him to return to the impenetrable cocoon he'd woven for himself.

Shamefully, she recognized that her love for Nick, for far

too long, had indeed been insisting on its own way.

Slowly, she slid down onto the floor next to him, picked up Galuppi, and laid the cat on the rug. Unfathomable, undefinable emotion directed her fingers to trace the indentations of his cheek.

The words came slowly. "My dearest, dearest Nick. I never could have known—I had no idea, honestly. I regret so deeply that I've brought you to the point where you felt you had to disclose all these painful things to me. I've been selfish and cruel—but not intentionally. Nick, you have to believe I never meant to be cruel."

"You don't have to tell me that, Claire."

"How wrong I've been from the start—beginning with the briefcase incident. Despite my best efforts, I've brought you nothing since we met but frustration, expense, inconvenience, and anguish."

"That isn't true at all. You've brought me joy, a type of joy I hadn't experienced since—since I was a kid, I guess. To have been acquainted with someone as adorable, talented, and fascinating as you, Claire, and as perceptive and decent—well, our time together has provided me with great pleasure. And fun! I'm thrilled that you love me, and I'd marry you in an instant if things were different. No Henri or wealthy impresario or any three-hundred-pound wrestling coach here at State would stand in my way."

"Nick, I'd give my life, I really would—I'd give up my music, everything—if I could wipe away the frustrations of your life. I'd gladly open your doors and windows and put out the fearful fires. . . ."

He pressed his arm closely around her, his biceps taut and firm, and so comforting. "I appreciate those words, Claire." He tousled her hair. "Now I'm going to go out into that kitchen of yours and rustle up some soup, coffee, lemonade, or something."

He got up, and she did too, though her head ached as she did so.

"No, Nick—*I'm* going to do that. There's chocolate cake and ice cream in the freezer, and I have some rather exotic spiced tea and—"

"My limitations do *not* include getting ice cream or cake from the freezer or fixing a cup of tea. Claire, don't you believe I can do these things for you?"

"Of course I believe you can. I *know* you can. You can do almost everything. But tonight I want to do this myself because I'd like things to be special. Besides, there's something else I want you to do. Select a CD of mellow music and play it for us. We'll eat right in here."

"I'd rather you just relax on the sofa and let me—"

"I have a Belgian lace cloth for this side table. It'll be elegant. Then after we've eaten, Nick, I'm going to take my medication; I'm getting pain in my jaw—it's becoming severe."

"That's because you're overdoing. You've been through a lot of trauma, and you should be resting."

"Not right now, because I want to plan a tiny party for us. Listen to me carefully. After we've eaten, as I said, I'm going to take my medication, and you're going to hold me in your arms—those strong muscles of yours are going to hold me until. . ."

He was looking down at her with questioning but patient eyes. "I've discussed all this so thoroughly, Claire. This is not the way to go."

"I want your arms around me, Nick," she went on determinedly. "I'll behave myself like a good little girl—no flirtations, no teasing, no come-ons. I'll let the medication take effect, and I'll fall asleep. I'll fall peacefully to sleep in your arms." She began to find the words difficult to say. "And, Nick, when I wake up, you'll be gone. Sometime in the night you'll get up and leave. Because. . .because, my dearest, if there's one pain I can't bear, it's seeing you walk out of my life again."

He bit his upper lip. Then he rubbed his forehead with his forearm. "All right," he said, lowering his arm, "if that's what you want."

"It's the only way I can let you go—for good. And, Nick, I promise, I really do, not to bounce my way into your world again." She trembled with the awful chill of these words. "I'll never storm your private barricades."

"Claire. . ."

"You can send me all the forms I have to sign regarding Porter—I'll sign them and send them right back. And if I ever need to get in touch with you for any reason, I'll do it through Jim. Should our paths cross, you have my word I won't lose my cool or embarrass you. Now I'm going to get our snack ready." She attempted to generate a sprightly air. "Act the DJ, please, and select a CD from the stereo cabinet."

He pulled her to him, turning her head to his. He leaned down and kissed her hair. Then he rested his head against hers and spoke softly into her ear, "Darling Claire, my sweet love, I'll do exactly as you wish. But I want you to know, as you fall asleep tonight, that in my thoughts I'll be holding you as my own, all of my life."

fourteen

Claire's June 6 arrival in Paris for her annual eight weeks with Henri and Yolande failed to raise her spirits sufficiently for her to recover from the trauma of losing Nick. She hadn't spent more than a few days with them before Henri disclosed his alarm about her appearance and lack of enthusiasm.

"You're not well, Claire-Therese. Yolande and I will have to outdo ourselves to put that sparkle back in your eyes. There's a Cezanne exhibit at the Louvre, a recital at Sacre Coeur, a—"

"Oh, Henri, I'm not up to all that. I've barely unpacked."

From the living room window, the tip of the Eiffel Tower reflected the setting sun over neighborhood rooftops. Below, on the street heading toward the Bois, autos scurried in and out of lanes, honking a welcome to the tantalizing Paris evening.

Claire's thoughts slipped back to Nick. *What time would it be at Everettsville right now? Two o'clock,* she calculated.

She pictured him walking through the new complex and down the catwalks of the old. In Paris, purple twilight descended on well-dressed people, a great contrast to the characters who walked past Nick in those awful cell blocks.

"*Chérie,* you are ill," Henri remarked. "You should see a doctor."

She shook her head, "No, I don't need a doctor." Tears she couldn't control beaded in her eyes as she turned around to face her kind family friend.

His expression told her he'd stumbled on the truth.

"You're in love, aren't you," he said.

She took several deep breaths to gain composure. "It was nothing more than a mere interlude."

He walked over to her and touched her eyes with his hand-kerchief. "Interludes do not create such havoc in the eyes of the accomplished Claire-Therese Rossiter, eyes I've observed since you were a child. Wouldn't it help to talk about it? Perhaps there is some way I can help."

"Talking is therapeutic, yes, but in this case, so difficult."

Henri guided her into a chair. Sitting on the adjacent couch, he listened attentively as she described her friendship with Nick.

At the mention of Nick being an amputee, Henri's eyes widened in shock. "An amputee. How did this happen?"

"An explosion while he was a student at Annapolis," Claire explained. "He refuses to consider marriage at all—and it's destroying me. I love him so much." The sobs surged up from her chest and soon convulsed her.

"*Ma petite amie*—how sad for you, for him as well.

"Where did you encounter this man? Is he a fellow professor? He can't be a musician, or. . ."

He paused, his eyes narrowing. "Wait a minute. Last fall, at your first recital of the season—at Lincoln Center. That good-looking prison warden came backstage with sumptuous roses—the warden whose briefcase you swiped by mistake. I remember that you were euphoric when you saw him. But he isn't an amputee—or is he?"

She tossed her head back and looked at the ceiling. "Yes, he's the guy."

"Oh, how tragic. He's a fine-looking chap—such a strong face. What a calamity. But, Claire-Therese, exceptional men and women often find solutions for the impossible. If there's some way I can help you and your noble friend, the warden. . ."

"My sweet Henri. . ." With tenderness she clasped his hand tightly. "There's no way—we can only hurt him further. Although he loves me, he believes we shouldn't see each other again. I reluctantly agreed. That's why I need a change of scenery so much this summer—my visit here and, next week, a few hours in Switzerland with Madame Bouchard, my childhood teacher."

"Personally, I don't think that you should traipse off to

Montreux—by train alone. I'm worried about you, now more than ever, with this unhappy experience weighing on your spirit. I'd be glad to drive—"

"Henri, I'll manage fine. Besides, it's only for a couple of days. Then I'll be back here in Paris once again for almost two months before I head home to the States."

&

Friday, as the train drew near Montreux, the familiar mountains appeared like roly-poly circus bears cavorting one on top of the other. They generated in her the joyful anticipation she needed to lighten her spirit.

Once in the city itself, she sat beside the lake to soak up the fairy-tale view. Across the iridescent water stood Byron's Castle of Chillon, famous as a prison for a family of patriots.

Unlike Everettsville, this prison stood surrounded by alpine magnificence.

Yet, *inside* this idyllic castle, Claire knew, lay dark dungeons more depressing than anything at Everettsville. Nick would find the castle's cells professionally intriguing.

She longed to share the castle with Nick, as well as picturesque Montreux. All of it, the quaint awninged buildings and the welcoming cafes and shops.

After settling in at the hotel, she went downstairs and asked the concierge to arrange for a car rental the next day to drive to Madame Bouchard's well-known school.

To her surprise, the concierge informed her the school didn't exist any longer. Instead, it had become a retreat center. She handed Claire a brochure that described the center, established by Madame Bouchard with assistance from such individuals as the nationally famous Austrian mezzo-soprano Gretl Schutt and shipping tycoon Giovanni Cambini.

That evening, when she phoned Henri to report that all was well, she couldn't control her excitement about visiting the center. "It's a Christian community, Henri—ecumenical, from what I gather—and well-known among the intelligentsia on the Continent."

"Claire, please change your mind," he implored. "Your Madame Bouchard's at least eighty. Her mind may be failing."

A grin engulfed Claire's face. "I sincerely doubt it. Under the circumstances, I want to see her more than ever."

"Claire-Therese, may I remind you, you're already on the downswing into melancholy about this amputee you're in love with. Do you think it sensible to waste time listening to a senile old woman ruminate in a smelly cloister about heaven and angels? You better get out of there and on the train back. . ."

"Not a chance," she declared. "I'm off to heaven and angels."

❧

What an excursion into nostalgia for Claire to drive up the familiar mountain highway to the old school. At every turn in the road, a pine tree or rock formation joined the wind in calling out hello. The mountains hugged her to them. Chalets curtsied in recognition.

Her meeting with Madame Bouchard exceeded all expectations. The frail, white-haired teacher hugged her with arms that yet had youthful strength as she ushered Claire into the familiar library.

"Claire-Therese, I was delirious with excitement when you called from Montreux to tell me you were coming to see me." She spoke in French, as did Claire. "A treat—a blessing—to enrich my day."

She pelted Claire with kisses as she continued, "I'm so eager to talk to you, and to hear you play for me. It has been too many years since I've seen you."

Nothing *had* changed since Claire's graduation. Every piece of furniture, including the ornate upright piano, was in the same place.

"So, what will it be? Mozart? Chopin?" asked the woman.

Claire raised her hands in obedient acquiescence. "Mozart? How will Mozart do?"

"Wonderfully."

Claire sat on the leather tufted bench and began a rondo that readily came to mind. Her mentor leaned against the side of the upright, her eyes bathing Claire with affection.

After the last note was played, Claire could see tears in those eyes.

"Claire-Therese, oh, my dear child, that was sublime," she crooned. "You are every bit as accomplished as the reports. Play something else, please."

"Only one more selection. There's so much to talk about. So many things for you to tell me. I must spend time listening to *you*."

The woman shrugged her shoulders and nodded yes.

Claire began the downward passages of a Bartok favorite, a vigorous, showy piece that she knew would satisfy as a finale.

With the last resounding chord echoing through the room, she rose from the bench and embraced the old teacher, who was visibly shaken by the power of the music.

They moved to two needlepoint chairs and sat down side by side.

"Now tell me, why did you give up the school?" Claire asked.

The woman described how individuals throughout Europe had felt the need to establish a center where they could join together in prayer for discernment—discernment to ameliorate the traumas of a hostile and chaotic world.

Madame Bouchard took a moment to squeeze Claire's hand in sweet friendship. "Too long we've neglected examining the Lord's purposes," she declared. "And our planet is in peril because of this neglect. People are crying out for altruistic role models who can help them find solutions for inequality and injustice.

"James 1:17 says: 'Every good and perfect gift is from above, coming down from the Father of the heavenly lights. . . .' Think of that—*every* good gift, such as your enormous musical ability."

Fingering back a wide swath through her short, uncoiffed white hair, Madame Bouchard proceeded, "The retreat program here was rather like a thunderbolt from the Holy Spirit that touched many individuals at the same time. Together, we turned this spot into an ecumenical Christian community. Oh, the blessings the Lord Jesus has showered on us. Each day we witness manifestations of His love. Like your coming into my life once again."

Claire looked back up into her teacher's face, which reflected a radiance that defied description.

Getting up from the chair, Claire walked to the west window, which framed splendor unsurpassed anywhere else on earth. Instead of feeling intimidated by the grandeur of the landscape, so illustrating God's mighty handiwork, she was overwhelmed by a realization of her value in God's eyes.

"Nick," she spoke softly to herself. "Oh, my precious Nick, is this it? Is the Lord really knocking at the door of my life to come in? Oh, I want You to do so, dear Lord Jesus. Forgive me for my neglect of You and for my selfish offenses. I need Your grace in my life."

A serenity settled upon Claire, promising a mystical bond between Nick and herself—and God—that oceans, mountains, and walls could never sever, no matter where her steps would take her in the future.

Blinking away tears of joy, she turned back to Madame Bouchard.

"You are one of us in the Spirit, I think," the woman said, "anointed by the Holy Counselor."

Claire smiled a yes, the tears flowing copiously. It was beyond words, this experience.

❧

Dinner in the community was simple fare, served buffet style to about fifty men and women in the large dining room. All appeared comfortable with the routine of the community, enthusiastically committed to its overriding policy—namely, that five weeks of every year be tithed to God, ideally one week in prayer at Montreux and four in "foot washing" service to the poor or infirm.

An Italian banker at her table had worked as a laborer

building septic tanks in Sicily. One of the writers had manned a London ghetto youth center.

"This way of life is not for everyone," said the banker, Signor Alessandro Galdieri, "but for us, it is the answer. We have been richly endowed, most of us, with families, money, and skills. But God calls us to assist the less fortunate. Our community here helps us focus on the area that commitment will take."

After dinner, as they headed for a chapel service, Signor Galdieri took her aside. "Even tonight, your being here, Ms. Rossiter, is in the nature of a spectacular blessing. At least, I think it *may* be. Following a phone call this very afternoon, I find myself in need of a musician."

"Surely not *this* musician," Claire replied, amusement in her eyes.

Signor Galdieri shrugged his shoulder, a beguiling smile on his face. "Quite possibly. I back a ballet company in Torino, which will be touring the United States next spring—it's opening in Houston. A protégé of mine, a highly skilled young ballerina of exceptional promise, was collaborating with an elderly composer on the subject of the poem, "Pippa Passes," by Robert Browning.

"If you recall, the poem deals with the little Italian factory girl whose cheerfulness alters the lives of many prominent citizens of Asolo."

"I do remember a bit about that poem, yes. It's a gem."

"The theme's especially engaging for this troupe because it employs an Italian subject immortalized by Browning, who made his home in Florence. I received word earlier today that the composer has suffered a stroke and cannot continue work on the ballet. Your success on the concert stage is well-known. And your comment over dinner that you have quite a few weeks yet of vacation leads me to wonder if you aren't the one the Lord has selected to help us out. We must go into production and rehearsal in two weeks' time."

Claire was prepared to give Alessandro Galdieri her customary expression of gentle dismissal, followed by the words,

"I'm sorry, but. . ." Then she checked herself. This was the very thing Nick thought she *should* be doing. If he were there, he'd be pushing her to accept the commission.

Her hesitancy caused the gentleman to speak further. "I know you will want to pray about this."

He paused and took a card from his wallet. Handing it to her, he continued. "I find myself in such a corner right now, I am behaving more impulsively than manners would dictate. The score is almost finished—only a *pas de deux* is yet to be written, plus, perhaps, some polishing needed on the whole." His sentences spilled out, his eagerness to have her aboard anything but subtle. "Naturally, you and the original composer would be listed as collaborators on the score."

"As a matter of fact, Signor Galdieri," she responded, "I have done some accompanying for the dance, so I do have an understanding of the type of music you need. But you're right when you say I must think about it—er, pray about it, if you will. Yes, I do need to do some praying. I'll give you my answer tomorrow morning."

When she phoned Henri the next day, she told him she had *accepted* an astonishing offer from a Signor Galdieri of Turin.

His reaction surprised her. "Alessandro Galdieri's one of the most influential men in the Po Valley, and you're telling me he was up on the mountaintop praying?"

"Yes, he's one of the many luminaries up there."

"Praying?"

"Yes, praying. Actually, Signor Galdieri believed I was the answer to his prayer."

"This is all very bewildering to me. But all I can say, Claire-Therese, is if this ballet comes off to rave reviews in Houston, I, myself, may fall on my knees." She could hear him chortling as he said this.

"Consider it done," she laughed back. With prayer, she now knew, even Henri on his knees might become a reality.

fifteen

Within days of the mountaintop meeting with Signor Galdieri, Claire found herself ensconced in a spacious apartment in Turin. The ballet production staff had provided her with a computer and a fine grand piano—the piano not only necessary for composing ballet music, but also for the practice required for her fall tour.

"Nick would never believe these palatial quarters," she gasped when she first beheld her surroundings. "A prison cell it is not."

In the ensuing weeks, collaboration with the ballerina Gina Vitale and the ailing composer, Guido Fardisi, proved to be virtually trouble free.

Watching Gina execute steps to the music left Claire incredulous, overcome with the realization that the fine performance unfolding before her was the result of her efforts—hers, Guido's, Gina's—and the Lord's.

And Nick's as well. At Madame Bouchard's she had almost sensed him prompting the yes she gave to Signor Galdieri.

Prayer indeed had caused this startling adventure to happen. Each day she asked the Holy Spirit to breathe His song into the music. To her surprise, melody upon melody, cadence upon cadence came from within, and made their way to her fingers, the piano, and eventually to the computer.

Rehearsal went on even as final drafts were being sent for copyright and printouts. Claire found herself caught up in the ebullience of the dedicated troupe, hardly willing to call it quits even when sessions continued well past midnight.

Signor Galdieri was jubilant, more than ever convinced God had sent Claire to him. He agreed with Gina that when the ballet was finally staged in Houston the results would be "dazzling."

Dazzling! Could a ballet she had helped compose actually be dazzling? It seemed that might be so.

"Next summer," Signor Galdieri proposed, "we shall want you back with us again, my dear young friend for a work based on the life of St. Francis. With much symbolism—dancers as birds, animals, and the like. Over the winter, you will put down all the tunes that pop into your head. Fax them on to me. I foresee for you, sweet lady, a most remarkable career."

Already plans were made for Claire's trip to Houston in May for the opening night, a gala Henri and Yolande planned to attend. Jim and Peg might be there too. But not Nick.

She debated about contacting him in what certainly had to be an exceptional occurrence. But with misgiving, she decided no; it was up to Jim and Peg to tell him about the ballet opening.

After the show's video became available, she'd give Jim an extra one to send to Nick.

She'd do that. But nothing more.

❧

Because of the extended weeks in Turin, Claire returned to the States facing a ferocious schedule. She had no regrets—the experience had proved to be exhilarating. But the project had forced her to squeeze a week of business into an afternoon.

The morning she landed, after the flight from Paris, she took a cab from the airport shuttle drop-off in the city to meet with her agent. There were loose ends about the fall tour—papers to sign, dates to be double-checked.

As the taxi snaked through the city traffic, she had time to lean back and assess the life-transforming weeks she'd just spent in Turin.

Sitting in the cab, Claire tried to organize her thoughts. There would be no lessons. Not till spring semester because the concert tour was so ambitious. Seven, eight hours of practice a day would be minimum to hone the Chopin E Minor Concerto—plus several encore selections—by October.

On October 11, she'd travel to Milwaukee for three day's

rehearsal with the Great Lakes Philharmonic, which would make the tour with her.

The six weeks ahead would be devoted to lonely practice once again, with no hope of ever duplicating that tour de force in Cincinnati.

How much more enjoyable it would be to remain in Turin, watching the ballet evolve into a polished, professional production. Or even just to return to the campus and take things easy for a month, rusticating on Regent Street with Galuppi, possibly experimenting with new musical ideas that even now arabesqued through her brain.

For weeks the ballet had been pleasurably enervating, erasing thoughts of Nick much of the time—or at least blurring them. Blurring them was more accurate. They were still there.

Returning to New York brought them painfully into focus.

Just a dozen or so blocks ahead was good old Lincoln Center. She could almost hear Nick's voice repeating that phone conversation with his ridiculous comment about reciting the Gettysburg Address in one meeting. She smiled painfully.

Had she loved him then? Or had she even loved him at the courthouse, listening to his evaluation of Zimblatz?

Had she ever not loved Nick? That was more to the point. And would there be a time in the uncharted future when she'd stop loving him?

The cab wove through the financial district, traffic all but impassable during lunch hour, jaywalkers darting in front of the cars at every stoplight.

She could take no time for lunch. As soon as she finished with her agent, she'd get her car at the garage leased by Henri's company. Then on up the thruway to campus and home.

Tomorrow—and all the tomorrows in the foreseeable future—would be devoted to nothing but practice, with only interruption for prayer. Prayer had now become an essential part of her day.

Even her visits with Jim and Peg would have to be infrequent. She'd get over to see them with the little remembrances she'd brought from Europe, yes, but evenings at Gleasons' could not be a regular part of her weekly calendar.

By January, this tour would be behind her. Never again would she plan something so arduous and all-consuming. After it was over, she'd direct her musical energies into teaching and composition.

While the traffic halted at an unfamiliar intersection, Claire noticed to her right a maze of high rises that appeared to be a hospital center. *Which one?* she asked herself.

Then she saw the sign. Davis Memorial.

Davis Memorial? She'd read about Davis Memorial in a recent news magazine. World-famous, Davis Memorial Hospital was noted for orthopedics, including artificial limb rehab. Why hadn't she ever seen it before?

The answer was simple. Before she'd met Nick, orthopedic hospitals held no interest for her.

In that complex right now there would be patients like Nick, adjusting to the trauma of amputation—young men, women, kids even, whose whole future seemed bleak.

As the cabby stopped for a traffic light, Claire had the overwhelming urge to get out and go into that hospital. Was that why the light seemed to take so long to change? Was the Holy Spirit telling her to go in there NOW?

No, she decided. The day was much too busy as it was.

And what would she do if she did go in? Stare with curious eyes at those disabled individuals, only adding to their discomfort, as she had to Nick's? Without skills or training what could she do to ease their adjustments to life?

Still the inner voice seemed to be telling her she could learn. But learn what?

Learn everything! How a prosthesis was affixed to the arm, plus the rudimentary steps an amputee would take in manipulating the prosthesis. She would observe the frustrations that would occur—and how to help a patient handle them. She could learn a thousand things.

Why did she desperately want to learn these things if she

had no intention of seeing Nick again or meeting up with guys like him? Ah, but her subconscious still clung to straws that cruelly suggested a future encounter with him.

She mustn't permit such thoughts to take hold. Unless—and this might well be true—unless knowing Nick could be a springboard to working with other kids and grown-ups who needed encouragement, hope, and discovery of the purpose God had for their lives.

There must be a program at Davis Memorial for volunteers, the inner voice continued.

"I'm sorry, Lord, it just isn't on my agenda for today," she whispered. "Next year, I might be able to fit it in." Yes, next year she could give it a whirl.

With the light green, the cab surged forward, and headed northwest to the theater district, leaving Davis Memorial behind.

➤

Her agent, Stan Frolich, was on the phone when she stepped into his office. He smiled sheepishly, indicating she should take a seat. As he talked to the other party, his smile turned into a grimace. Putting his hand over the receiver, he mouthed a comment, "I've got some lousy news that's not going to make your day."

Finally hanging up the phone with an exasperated goodbye, he turned to her. "Today I'm on the ropes. That call's from a violinist who just broke his arm. Playing croquet! He's scheduled for five recitals in New England, starting in three weeks. Isn't that beautiful!"

"Poor guy," Claire responded.

"Yeah. How 'bout poor me? Okay, now we turn to your tour." He zipped through his computer to her readout and then thumbed through a pile of folders, pulling out hers. He slammed it on the desk in disgust. "You won't believe this, Ms. Rossiter. The orchestra scheduled for your tour has gone on strike."

Claire sat forward, her eyes wide. "Has what?"

"Two days ago the Great Lakes Philharmonic went on strike. No rehearsals—nothing. The orchestra's canceling the tour."

"Can they do that?"

"They've done it! Somewhere there's fine print about union benefits that aren't being honored. Lawyers have been called in. I only have to pick up the pieces with the cities on the tour and unruffle their feathers."

Claire began to snicker. Then that snicker became a full-fledged, shoulder-shaking laugh. "This is unreal."

She slapped a palm against her forehead and leaned back in her chair.

A bewildered Stan Frolich stammered, "It's shattering for you, Ms. Rossiter, I know that. You were counting on this tour. I'm sorry for you, I really am—but, bu—why under the sun are you laughing?"

"Because it had to happen. This concert tour was never meant to be. I have better things to do."

"No, wait a minute, Ms. Rossiter, we have no intention of leaving you dangling. One of the other orchestras we're considering might be able to include you. We can get you work—it's just going to take some juggling."

She sat up and tried to manage a serious demeanor. "Do I have to perform somewhere to fulfill my contract? I mean, legally, is it possible to just not perform anywhere at all?"

"Under these circumstances, yup, since you didn't initiate the action—you're within your rights to do that. In fact, you'll be paid a fee of five thousand dollars sitting at home doing zilch. But you'll want exposure somewhere. You're just getting things off the ground professionally. And you're good."

"Five thousand dollars would take care of me fine for several months. Stan, over the summer I became involved in composing ballet music. It's been lucrative as well as satisfying. Also I'll be back teaching at State in January, so money isn't tight right now. In addition, something else has come up—nothing to do with music—that I'd like to explore."

"You mean you're not about to sue me?"

"Hardly. Accept this for what it's worth; God doesn't want me to go on this tour. He wants me to channel my energies into something else for a few months. Let me make a suggestion."

"I'm all ears."

"Are the violinist's recitals in major concert halls?"

"No. Mainly at universities and art museums, but well-respected places on the recital circuit."

"Fine. I could easily handle them. And I won't accept another penny beyond the five thousand you're giving me."

"I couldn't let you do that. The violinist was going to get. . ."

"Sure, you could. I have to practice every day, anyway, to keep up my dexterity. So, I'll resurrect some of my old standbys. What can an audience expect from a substitute?"

Stan eyed her for a moment. Then his face broke into a canvas of smiles. "I don't know about God having something else for you to do—but I know this much, you've been a boon and a blessing to me today. I dreaded facing you. And look how it's turned out. Yeah, I could use you for those recitals. Boy, could I."

She grabbed her purse and stood up. "Stan, just fax me the details about the recitals. I'll keep in touch. But right now, you'll have to excuse me if I run." She reached for his hand.

He stood and shook hers. "Run, lady, run. You have yourself a deal. And—er, boatloads of thanks."

☙

Tension, confusion about where she would go and to whom she would speak, bombarded Claire as she entered the spacious lobby of Davis Memorial Hospital. A receptionist informed her a nurse-administrator named Sandra Hunt headed the staff on the floor dealing with amputation. She directed her to the elevator which would take her to that floor.

Though professional in appearance and demeanor, Sandra Hunt received her warmly. Claire felt at ease telling her about her association with the university, the cancellation of her concert tour, and explaining her reasons for wanting to volunteer at Davis. "A very dear friend is a bilateral amputee. I'd like to think my volunteering here would be a tribute to him. Since my fall tour just got canceled a few moments ago, I have all this extra time this fall. What better way to spend it than to help you out here at Davis."

Nearly as an aside, Claire mentioned her ballet project.

Sandra Hunt shook her head in amazement. "You've written a ballet? That's amazing."

"I've collaborated on one, yes."

"On this floor, Ms. Rossiter—er, Claire, we don't take hands for granted. I'm moved by the fact that your capable fingers will be available to assist others to achieve manual dexterity. That means so much to me."

As she got up to leave, Claire handed Sandra Hunt her card. "I absolutely mustn't keep you any longer, Mrs. Hunt. Let me give you my card so you can reach me."

The woman walked around the desk and held Claire's fingers, almost reverently. "I'll be calling you soon—in a day or so."

Claire weighed the comment she was about to make, then boldly aired it, "It just dawned on me, you may know my friend—well, anyway, my wonderful amputee friend, Nick Van Vierssen."

Sandra Hunt's eyes lit up. "I do know him. Actually, I've only met him at a conference we had last year. I'm sure he doesn't remember me. Why, he's a charming man, so well-adjusted to his handicap."

"Not really all that well-adjusted, Mrs. Hunt. At least when it comes to marriage. Although he's admitted he loves me, he doesn't believe I could cope with his disability if we were married. We've decided not to see one another."

"I'm sorry to hear that. He's a fine and capable man. But now that I've met you, I'd say you are equally fine and capable."

"He told me I'd be appalled by his private life."

"I'm not that sure you would be, but Mr. Van Vierssen

would know what would be best for him."

"Second best might be helping the folks on this floor. . . giving them confidence that they can reach for much more in this world than they expected they could when their disability first occurred."

Sandra Hunt squeezed Claire's hand as they walked to the elevator. "A noble idea. I'll feel privileged to help you in this effort."

&

Sandra Hunt was as good as her word, phoning Claire within the week. Outfitted with appropriate slacks and tops—and substantial shoes, Claire reported for duty at Davis Memorial on September 10.

sixteen

The first week at Davis, Claire wondered, as a new Christian, if she'd misread God's directing her into this volunteer venture after all. Initially, she was assigned to a practical nurse who supervised temperature-taking, baths, and basic patient needs. Simple tasks under normal circumstances, but when done with amputees, Claire found the exercise emotionally draining.

Viewing for the first time the severed stumps—their discolorations along surgical closures—left her limp. Several times she was forced to leave a patient's room and go out into the hall to fight back tears.

The idyllic mountains of Montreux seemed so far away. Not infrequently, God seemed far away as well. In these moments when her faith foundered she clung to the psalmist's words: "Show me your ways, O Lord; teach me your paths."

Adding to her anxiety was the realization that Nick must have gone through the agony of phantom pain in addition to the helplessness resulting from his lost hands. So preoccupied was she about what Nick must have gone through, she couldn't get to sleep many nights.

By the end of the second week on duty, however, activities that weakened her the first few days became more or less routine. Still Claire knew she had yet to face the ultimate test: Unlike Nick, none of the patients she helped had lost both hands. Sandra Hunt assured her such a patient would appear on the scene eventually.

Ed Lytton was that patient.

He had been brought in by helicopter from upstate, a victim of a collapsed roof in an auto body shop. "Lytton's case is far from pleasant, Claire," said Sandra Hunt. "But I think you're ready to face it."

"Yes, Sandra, I'm ready," Claire insisted, her conviction shrouded in misgivings. "This is why I came to Davis in the first place."

"It's unlikely the emotional makeup of this man will be anything like that of your friend, Mr. Van Vierssen," cautioned Sandra.

"I understand that."

Sandra grasped her arm firmly. "He was airlifted here because he's made little progress and. . ."

Her words were blotted out by a bellowing voice from the room where they were heading. "Isn't there anyone—anyone at all out there—who can get in here and scratch my shoulder?" This was followed by an almost inhuman, primordial sound.

Sandra steadied Claire and gave her an encouraging smile as they entered the darkened room. Once her eyes became accustomed to the darkness, Claire witnessed the helpless man. He was lying flat on the bed, the prostheses already attached to his arms like tree limbs on a snowy field.

His head tossed spasmodically from side to side, the mouth clenched. The compassion that welled up in her throat made it impossible for Claire to say hello—cheerful or otherwise—to the man. Easy banter seemed to be out of place—almost sadistic. Yet it was this very approach that Sandra employed.

"Mr. Lytton," she said, "what a great day. Ms. Rossiter and I will remove your equipment. Then, you're going to trot yourself into that bathroom to shower yourself into respectability."

"Respectability? That's some kind of a joke, lady," he shouted at her. "Just scratch my back and get lost. I don't care if I rot to death."

"Well, I regret to tell you rotting to death isn't permitted. The Board of Health opposed that unanimously several decades ago," Sandra replied in a no-nonsense manner, opening the blinds and turning on the light. "We must protect our licensing. So right now the schedule says shower."

The man sputtered through grinding teeth as Sandra and Claire began removing the right Greifer. "In a week or so," said Sandra, "you'll be putting these on and taking them off by yourself. You'll be able to take showers by yourself whenever you wish."

"There's no way I'll be able to do that, and you know it," he answered bitterly.

"Oh, you'll be able to do all those things in a breeze, mark my word. Our shower stalls have nifty foot pedals rigged to the shower head—one to deliver sudsy flow, clear water from the other—just like a car wash. You'll have no trouble at all."

Claire stared at the man who lay before her, his torso now bared—the prostheses removed. Although his stumps were healing, there were still angry red lines where the staples had been. It was impossible to see anything of Nick in the man lying there. He certainly didn't possess Nick's handsome face with its infectious grin. Or Nick's stunning eyes, so often overflowing with merriment.

She couldn't imagine Nick's torso resembling Ed Lytton's sweat-soaked body that lay on the rumpled sheets.

As she looked at the man, all Claire could think of were scenes from movies about the Inquisition where a man was being stretched on the rack. She almost felt like a torturer, ready to turn the wheel that would take the victim over the edge into screaming insanity.

The helplessness and despair of this man overwhelmed Claire. She wanted to just hold Ed Lytton in her arms and rock him, as a mother would a newborn.

Sandra kept up a persistent patter, bringing Ed up on his feet and directing him to the shower. "I can't stand up and walk in there," he stormed. "I can't dangle these–these. . ."

" 'Stumps' is a word you'll have to get used to, Ed," said Sandra.

"All right. I can't dangle these stumps. It hurts like mad.

I tell you I can't walk in there." He added a stream of obscenities.

"In and out—just in and out. It'll give you such a boost," prodded Sandra.

In an overpowering instant, as Ed Lytton made his way to the shower, Claire saw the depth of Nick's private purgatory portrayed in graphic outline. That back and those shoulders could have been Nick's. The abbreviated, so unevenly severed handless arms—the male figure before her that stood so barbarously incomplete—was the Nick she had never seen.

Violent nausea churned up from her stomach. It took several deep breaths to attempt to keep it at bay.

"Sandra. . . ," she mumbled, "I–I have to leave. I. . ."

"Buzz for another nurse," mouthed Sandra. "I can manage until she arrives."

Claire rang the buzzer twice and then slipped from the room as decorously as possible. Once in the hall, she ran to the ladies' room "Lord, I'm not strong enough," she groaned. "I came here with pure intent, wanting to give these individuals a reason for living. But I can't rise above my love for Nick. Seeing the state Ed Lytton's in has destroyed my objectivity. I want so desperately to talk to Nick. . .to hold him to me, and to. . .Lord, I want to love him. In the deepest recesses of my being, I feel that all I'm doing here is to learn how to live with Nick, and I'm ashamed of that selfishness.

"Help me return to my original purpose in coming here. . . to provide assistance to any amputee, here or anywhere else. Help me to make the Ed Lyttons my priority, not Nick. Hard as it is for me to believe, I do think You—and Nick—would want me to do that. Help me honor my commitment to stay here until December and do my best."

ಜ

Despite great misgivings, she discovered as November approached, she could provide care plus encouragement to Ed Lytton. Taking cues from Sandra Hunt, she supervised and assisted him in putting on prostheses, using a spoon and fork to feed himself, and even playing cards with the help of a card tray.

Soon, Ed could handle many activities well. He could turn on the television, thumb through the pages of a book, play electronic games—scribble his name. In their conversations, Claire often made reference to her friend who was also an amputee, yet able to ski, play table tennis, and hold a responsible position in a prison.

Frequently, Ed asked her to read the Bible to him. He was particularly interested in the story of the man with the withered arm. "But I can't be healed like that," he said. "Do you expect me to believe God's going to paste my hands back on?"

"Isn't that really what He has done, Ed?" she replied with words that didn't seem to originate with herself. "Those prostheses are hands He has pasted back on. He's expecting you to learn to use the new hands He's given you—perhaps for a task you've never imagined for yourself."

Two other similar amputees became patients in late November. Jake, a sixty-year-old auto mechanic, was a tough fellow, a bachelor, whose sense of humor heroically got him through the first few days. Even though much of his conversation was crude, Claire admired his stoicism. But one remark he made proved unsettling to Claire. Over a game of electronic baseball, he said, "I'm sure glad I'm not married to a doll as pretty as you. I'd be bananas in a month. Not to have fingers to touch a wife like you, would be some kind of torture, sweetheart."

Her relationship with Sam, the other amputee, was equally jarring. So distraught was his wife over her husband's condition, she moaned, "What a cross to bear. I can't live with this situation. Sam used to be such a dynamic man. Coaching little league. Repairing things around the house. Now he's helpless and can't do anything."

Lunch with Sam's therapist further undermined Claire's optimism. "Forever and a day, spouses give amputees a bad time," she declared.

"Always?" asked Claire, trying to hide her emotions. Apparently Sandra Hunt hadn't told the staff about Nick and herself.

"Ninety-five percent of the time," added the therapist. "They complain too much or wait on their husbands hand and foot, so guys like Sam never gain sufficient skill with their prostheses to return to meaningful work. Some never keep up with their therapy. They give up totally."

Claire attempted a weak smile, her mood anything but cheerful.

&

Only a few more days remained for Claire at Davis once the Christmas season arrived. In the new year, the second semester would begin at State. She would resume a full schedule of lessons, and her volunteer stint would be over.

On December 17, the staff took her out to a surprise luncheon, presenting her with a charming plaque. Ed Lytton joined the celebration. His words of gratitude for her assistance over some "rough days" touched her immensely. He had turned his life over to Christ, he'd announced. Everyone at the dinner commented on his newborn optimism and self-assurance.

With reluctance and sadness, she approached Sandra Hunt's office on her last day to say good-bye. Sandra embraced her warmly. "Your stint here comes to a close, Claire. But our friendship will continue."

"I'm only sorry I can't help you on a regular basis next semester, Sandra. My training here has been worthwhile, not only for me, but for others too, apparently."

"You'll be back to see us often, I hope. You and Mr. Van Vierssen."

Claire took Sandra's hand as they walked to the elevator.

"You're an individual who well deserves the exciting future that lies ahead for you." Not sure how she would respond to Sandra about the future, she let the nurse go on. "You have the success in your music to look forward to, as well as your reunion with that superb man you love. I do hope I'll at least receive an announcement of your wedding."

The elevator opened and they got on. Fortunately, they were alone. Claire turned to her friend. "Sandra, I don't know how to say this to you—but, ah, I've decided it is wisest to honor my promise not to get in touch with Nick Van Vierssen."

Dropping her hand from Claire's grasp, Sandra looked at her incredulously. "You can't mean that. How can you deny that fine man a chance to know what you've done?"

"I've grown much wiser these past few months."

"Have you? You'd call this decision a wise one? What happened to the Holy Spirit's propelling you to this hospital?"

"I misread God's direction for me, that's all. He did have a plan, yes. He wanted to prove to me that Nick does know best. A satisfactory marriage is all but impossible for the men I've met here. I made a promise to Nick. I'm sticking to it."

The elevator opened. Taking Claire's arm firmly, Sandra directed her into an empty lounge adjacent to the lobby, forcing her to sit down on a sofa. "You've been strongly influenced by a very negative individual—someone on my staff?"

"Not entirely."

"I think you have, Claire. It's my opinions that my conclusions have as much if not more merit than those of anyone in this hospital. I'll readily admit that I have seen unsavory consequences of amputation. Suicides, insanity, divorce—you name it. But I've also seen men and women go out of here to live useful lives. I've seen some marriages work, sometimes better than they ever did before."

Sandra began to talk faster and in a more vehement tone. "Last year, a farmer with several young children went back to his family and made an excellent adjustment to both family and farm. He and his wife were tremendous people. But so are you, Claire, and from my observation of Mr. Van Vierssen at that conference, so is he."

"He's tremendous, all right, Sandra. But you can't compare his situation with that farmer's. The farmer was already married. Nick would prefer to live his life alone. Keep this in mind as you. . ."

"Let me finish," Sandra interrupted with great urgency. "Just bear with me, and let me finish. There's no way in the world you can convince me Mr. Van Vierssen is content without you. I'm sure he's agonizingly lonely. What young buck wouldn't be, after being in your company?

"Certainly you and he will have frustrations, yes, but you are both mature enough to cope with them, especially now that you've experienced so much here."

"Sandra, we'll face hurdles not covered here."

"Of course you will. But amputees aren't the only folks to have hurdles in a marriage. Everyone has a handicap of some sort—physical, emotional, educational, spiritual. Married couples must have the patience to alleviate the pain caused by these disabilities.

"If God hadn't given me my Bob," Sandra continued, "who has a few annoying emotional handicaps of his own— if I didn't have him and my two daughters to go home to, I couldn't do this job. Please reconsider your decision. At least give Mr. Van Vierssen himself the opportunity to reevaluate the situation in light of your efforts here. Give him that Christmas gift he so deserves."

Claire shook her head. "No, Sandra, I'm not going to do that. You're correct when you said I do have a plateful of exciting projects ahead. And I want you to know that the time I've spent here has been valuable to me. I wouldn't have missed it for the world."

"I'm heartbroken," said the woman. "I'm truly heartbroken about this."

"Please don't be, Sandra. With the Lord's help, I'll sever Nick from my life and adjust to my amputation from him, just as he and the patients here have had to adjust to theirs."

Claire got up from the sofa. From her purse she gave Sandra a tiny gift wrapped in green Christmas foil. Then she reached over and kissed her. "Thank you so much, Sandra—

for teaching me how to assist amputees, and for giving me enough of an insider's view of their complicated world—so that finally I can let Nick go."

seventeen

It was fortunate Claire had curtailed her activities at Davis when she did. On December 24, a five-inch snowfall made the driving hazardous.

Falling snow had enveloped the campus in a womb of white. With the students absent now for the holidays, an almost celestial quiet pervaded the ivory world beyond Claire's window.

She'd temporarily replaced the plum-colored plant with a good-sized crèche containing hand-carved figures purchased in Zurich many years ago.

On Saturday, she had attended a faculty dinner with Pete Crane from the physics department. So far the holiday season had been enjoyable.

Fortunately, there weren't many things on the agenda for the day. She could concentrate on a run-through of *The Messiah,* which she would accompany for Holy Redeemer Church at four o'clock, after which there was to be a reception at the dean's.

Tomorrow she'd be with Jim and Peg and their adorable children for Christmas dinner.

She strolled into the living room, her coral lounging robe swishing across the carpet. It was a lounging robe kind of morning. She scanned the cards on the mantel, many of them from students who'd achieved success in the world of music. It made her seem almost ancient to know that Billy Ramirez had joined the music faculty at UCLA, Doreen Tremont was touring in Brazil, and Deke Leavitt had his own jazz band in Miami.

Although it was nonsense to think of herself as middle-aged at twenty-eight, she did feel too elder-statespersonish for comfort.

Behind a tiny, tempting gift from the Poncelets, there was a card from Arnold Saxby, of all people, and one from Sandra Hunt and the Davis staff, flanked by poignant notes from Madame Bouchard and the ballet company.

Then there was Nick's card, even though she hadn't sent him one. Each time she passed the mantel, she had to pick it up to look at that distinctive signature with its long tail on the "k" that said so much. It was easy now, since her tenure at Davis, to picture him penning his name. She knew only too well how long it had taken him to learn to do it so skillfully with phony fingers. Or toes.

He had added a few scrawled words in pen. "Terrific news about the ballet. I'm thrilled for you."

Jim had told her he'd mentioned it to Nick.

Putting the card back on the mantel with the others, she went to the piano and let her fingers meander for a few thoughtful moments. There was no great need to open the music for *The Messiah*. She knew it well, but the choir director had noted a few special phrasings and crescendos. She opened to that masterful selection "For Unto Us," astounded, as always, by Handel's sublime genius, now more than ever thrilled by the message so eloquently conveyed. "Unto us a child is born." The Savior Child she now welcomed so fervently into her being.

Envisioning that Child in a stable, she thought about little Josh Gleason, so precious to his family. She wondered if she would have a child someday.

Even though she knew she would never marry Nick, she doubted she would ever care to bear anyone else a son.

Oh, what a boy Nick would have, with Nick's calm and empathetic authority mixed at all the right moments with relaxed levity. As she played the music, she yearned to meet that son—*his* son—*their* son.

Or a daughter. Nick's daughter would be kind, regal, and sensible. She well might have long, sun-speckled cascades of lovely hair—and maybe elegant sapphire eyes.

Claire ached to see these children.

The finale of the piece, with the four-voice parts building to that magnificent unison, illustrated majestically the power of the greatest Child who had ever lived—Jesus, the Son of God, the Messiah foreseen by Isaiah the prophet.

The music left her awed and breathless. It was so *over!*

A sudden strong breeze across her back proved she was no longer alone. She mustn't have closed the door tightly when she went to bed.

Tensely, she realized someone else was in the room. The wind from the opened front door caused a shiver to ripple down her spine. She was afraid to turn around.

Slowly, she pivoted.

Standing by the stairs near the front door was. . .*Nick!*

Her eyes must be tricking her. It had to be a figment of her imagination.

No, it was the real McCoy—Nick in the flesh, wearing his fine camel's-hair overcoat with the collar turned up, separating strands of the snow-sprinkled shock of windblown hair that framed his face, now ruddy-red from the snow and the blustery wind.

This time. . .oh, this time it had to be *forever*. He was smiling as if it were. His mouth was relaxed, his arms open to her.

She leaped from the bench, lifted the skirt of her robe, and ran into his arms. His crushing embrace told her all she needed to know. He had come to tell her he wanted to share her life as her husband.

He raised her face to his and kissed her, not with an anxious frenzy as he had before, but with the confident lips of a man who'd finally arrived home after a long journey.

He pulled away slightly.

"Nick, no," she cried. "Oh, my darling, don't let go of me yet. I've waited much too long for you to. . ."

"Let me at least take off my coat," he said with amusement in his eyes. "Will you permit me, please, to do that, you incorrigible, unpredictable little minx, you?"

"Just do it quickly."

He tossed the coat over the banister. Under a black, bulky knit sweater, she could see just the open collar of a red candy-striped shirt at his neck as she fell back against his chest again.

His lips found her cheeks, then her eyes, her hair. . .her lips.

"Not a trace of black and blue or green anywhere, is there?" he noted, laughing.

"No."

"No pain in the old jaw?"

"None."

"You're the most captivating woman. Has anyone besides Henri and a hundred newspaper critics ever told you that?"

"Does it matter if they have? When I hear it from you, that's all that counts. Nick, being with me *this* time means. . .?"

"Means I'm going to marry you, yes. And Claire, I'm going to make it all work out for us or die trying."

Putting his arm around her shoulder, he directed her into the living room. "What a beautiful crèche, Claire," he said, moving to the bay window to inspect it. "But you didn't throw out the plum-colored plant, I hope."

"Oh, never—it's in my bedroom. I'll never part with it. Can I get you something? A cup of coffee? Waffles? I can whip up waffles in. . ."

"The coffee'll be fine, but not just yet."

His arm still resting on her shoulder, he leaned against the window frame. She traced the lines of his face with the care she'd used handling the crèche figures.

"My darling, seeing you is a miracle," she said. "Thank God. . . . Oh, thank You, God. Nick, why did you change your mind?"

She moved back a few steps and studied his sensitive eyes, now filled with dancing glimmers of light that played affectionate games with her.

"You *were* right all along, Claire. God *absolutely* does want us together. He went so far as to send an angelic emissary into my life who related the most far-fetched story—about an individual who rearranged her schedule to work with amputees. By any chance, do you happen to know that saga, Claire?"

He fixed his eyes on hers and their souls touched.

"Jim must have been that emissary," she responded. "But how did he ever find out about Davis? I didn't let anyone on campus know about my work there."

Nick shook his head. "It wasn't Jim, but I'm glad it was *someone*. If I hadn't found out. . .Claire, it's horrifying to think I might never have found out! Is it possible you weren't going to tell me?"

"I'd made a promise to you, Nick. I decided to live up to that promise."

"But when you went to work at Davis, your intention was to let me know eventually?"

"Yes."

"And you felt God had directed you in that venture?"

"Yes."

"Then you changed your mind."

"I figured you'd been wise all along. So many of those patients *did* have wives who couldn't manage to—"

"But they didn't have *you*. I should have known with a woman like you, nothing is quite by the book. Anyone who plays Liszt as you do can accomplish anything."

"Right!" she said with dramatic bravado. "Now, you cruel ogre, tell me how you found out my secret. I bet you went to a conference and someone from Davis was there who happened to mention my name and. . ."

"No, there wasn't any conference." He paused, scowling dramatically. "This is a spellbinding story, but taxing on an empty stomach. Why don't you fix me that coffee so I'll be fortified and not apt to miss any of the juicy details?"

"You're a tease," she spouted in a scolding tone. "But in this case I'll be glad to oblige." She moved toward the kitchen. "Waffles, too?"

"No, just coffee—and maybe a piece of toast," he said, following her.

"The coffee's still hot," she said, feeling the pot on the coffee-maker. She poured a cup. "Cream and sugar?"

"Cream. I'll get it." He opened the refrigerator and took out the carton. Carefully he poured the cream. Instead of pity, she now looked upon this feat with a clinical awe. He was such a champ using his prostheses, she almost shouted out a hearty bravo.

She tossed slices of bread into the toaster.

From under the table, Galuppi came slinking out. He trotted up to Nick, nuzzling his leg.

"Galuppi, you remember me," Nick said, getting down on one knee and stroking the cat. "And you're glad to see me, too—what a nice welcome." He glanced up at Claire, caressing her with that look.

She still couldn't believe he was here in the kitchen with her.

Nick lifted the cat's mouth up to his ear.

"Galuppi tells me you didn't miss me at all," he joked. "You were too busy entertaining the men of the math department, romping most precipitously through logarithms and complex variables."

"Galuppi's a notorious liar," she retorted with a smirk.

He dropped the cat gently, and they took the coffee and toast into the living room.

"Now, no more stalling," she said, curling up next to him on the sofa. "Who told you about my work at Davis?"

"A wise individual named—Sandra Hunt!"

Claire stared at Nick in total surprise, as he smugly munched a piece of toast. "That's impossible. Sandra Hunt's a professional to the nth degree. She'd never. . ."

"Well, in this instance, I'm afraid she did. She thought this situation called for action on her part. Let me recap," he continued. "I was in my office yesterday morning, working on a report, when I got a call from a woman who sounded terribly ill-at-ease. When she said she was on staff at Davis, I figured she wanted me to give a talk or a demonstration, and I was prepared to say no. We've been so busy with hearings in Washington lately, I didn't feel up to adding an extra speaking engagement to the calendar."

He took Claire's hand in his Greifer, seeming to know it wouldn't upset her any longer. "The report I was writing took precedence over her call, I'm afraid, so I gave her only half an ear. During the conversation, I kept scanning my report and running some figures through my calculator. Then I heard her say something like, 'and this lovely girl is Claire Rossiter, a friend of yours.' "

He took several sips of coffee before he went on. "I bolted up in my chair, completely nonplused, and barked at that poor woman, '*Claire Rossiter?* Hold everything. Repeat that story again, please.'

"The woman sounded relieved to know I was at least interested, so she continued, much more confidently, to tell me how reluctant she'd been to phone, and that she hoped I'd forgive her for interfering in my private life. She'd never done anything like this before, she admitted. I assured her I was keenly interested in *all* the accomplishments of the celebrated Ms. Rossiter."

He paused a minute, shaking his head as his eyes searched the depths of hers. "But, darling Claire, I wasn't prepared for the disclosures she presented. I'm glad no one else was in my office at the time, because I lost control of myself. I covered the receiver, and broke down right there."

"Nick, oh, my dearest—it was uncanny that I came upon Davis. When I saw the place, I knew I *had* to go in there. It was imperative that I learn, that I observe firsthand what you've been through."

"I've been pigheaded, Claire. A pietistic idiot, never imagining any woman, least of all a talented person like you, could ever be in love with me enough to accept my limitations over the long haul."

Tenderly he raked a prosthesis through her hair. "Selfishly, I let my own pride interfere with a relationship that was orchestrated from the beginning by the Lord. Yesterday, when I realized how I'd hurt you by never comprehending the depth of your love, I was so ashamed. I've been a selfish, egotistical fool."

"Nick, you could never be selfish and egotistical."

"I *have* been, Claire, with you. Mrs. Hunt told me how you'd worked tirelessly on that floor, consoling families, feeding men and women—and doing a dozen other unpleasant tasks I can picture only too clearly."

He bit his lip in thought, then continued. "She told me you planned to tell me about your work 'through a friend.' Jim, I trust. Then, out of the blue, you changed your mind. She said she pleaded with you to reconsider. After many sleepless nights, she decided I should know. I assured her I certainly *should* know. In fact, I told her my gratitude knew no bounds. She'd provided me with a future on planet Earth I'd thought was well beyond my uniquely limited grasp. I promised her I'd thank her properly by taking her to dinner at the Gentilhomme Restaurant in the city—the sky's the limit—truffles, caviar, the works."

"Will I be included in that festive event?"

He wrinkled up his nose, as if he'd think about that. "Hmm, maybe, if I don't have you scrubbing floors eight hours a day to make my Dutch household spotless. I don't want to over-truffle you like Henri has."

She wrinkled her nose as well. "Thanks a *lot*."

He laughed heartily. "You'll be there."

"I'll give Sandra a piece of my mind, that appalling, dear, thoughtful, sensational woman." Tears flowed down Claire's cheeks—tears so expressive of her joy that she didn't want to wipe them away.

"As soon as Mrs. Hunt got off the phone," Nick continued, "I called the superintendent and told him I had to have three days off."

"Three days? We have three days together?"

"Yes."

"And the superintendent didn't mind?"

"He was so impressed by what you'd done at Davis, he *ordered* me to take off this morning. He said he'd see that all sally ports were covered, even if he had to work two shifts and have his family eat Christmas dinner in a prison mess hall. I didn't argue with him—just packed my bags early this morning and left before dawn. In fact, I got here at nine o'clock and waited around until I thought it was a decent enough hour to come to your door."

"Oh, no—you mean there were extra minutes we could have spent together?"

"A few."

"We can't waste any more minutes like that, my dearest."

He shook his head a few times, "No, we can't."

"Three whole days—it's heaven, or almost. But, Nick, there are complications today." She got up and walked to the piano to get a program. "I have a service this afternoon. The folks at Holy Redeemer Church are singing *The Messiah*. I'm the accompanist—they *really* need me."

She smiled with a trace of affected pain as she handed him the program.

He scanned it quickly, but returned his eyes to her. "I'd love to attend *The Messiah* on Christmas Eve. If you're the accompanist, it will be even more enjoyable."

"There's a reception at the dean's at seven. I should stop in for a minute or two."

"I'd like to meet the dean. In fact, I brought along my gray suit just for such an occasion."

She took a Greifer into both her hands. "Perfect. I can't wait for everyone to meet you—I'm so proud of you and the type of work you do. I love you so. Tomorrow I've planned to go to Jim and Peg's for dinner."

"Sensational. I don't think they'll mind at all if we celebrate our engagement with them."

"Jim will go into shock."

"He will, won't he?"

She became serious for a second. "But your parents, Nick;

don't you usually celebrate part of Christmas week with them?"

"Not always, no. Besides, I phoned them last night. They were ecstatic at hearing my news. My mother whispered a reverent, 'Hallelujah!' when I told her I was going to propose to the most magnificent girl on earth—someone famous, with a pair of hands that would more than compensate for mine in a marriage."

She smiled down at him. "Next year, we'll give them a grandchild," she murmured, barely audibly.

But he'd heard her. "Wait a minute now. That's rushing things a bit, isn't it? You don't want to have morning sickness for the opening of that ballet in Houston."

This made her chuckle. "Well, no, I guess that would be bad planning. But I'm not going to let ballets stand in my way forever. I'm getting very old, you know."

As if she were a little girl, his strong arms pulled her to him and sat her on his lap. He stretched out his legs on the sofa. "Yes, you're edging toward thirty, I bet—a veritable relic. Claire, it's beyond me that we're talking about children—*our* children. Me, a father to a child of yours! That's a responsibility too awesome to contemplate.

"Darling, coming up the walk this morning, I could hear your brilliant Handel. When I found the door unlocked, I just stepped in to what seemed to me a mirage. There you were, so incredibly lovely, sitting at the piano. I had to pause in wonderment, in acceptance of the fact that that magnificent creature loved me enough to go into hospital rooms and scrub stumps and scratch itches and brush away tears."

Tears were escaping his own eyes. "I've learned a mighty lesson these last dozen hours or so. You honestly love this miserable body of mine—a great deal more than I do. What's more, God loves me a lot more than I'd imagined. He's given you to me, to share my life. In His sight I'm pretty valuable, hands or no hands. Correct?"

"You're the most valuable human being alive, as far as I'm concerned."

"And that leads into what marriage is all about, Claire. Last night I reexamined Ephesians 5:28. Husbands should love their wives as their own bodies. It's a holy act to love you, to the best of my ability. But I have to love myself in the process."

She nodded.

"Claire, your foot-washing service to those patients at Davis was done for *me,* so I hope I'll have the good sense to rejoice on those occasions, which will certainly come up in our marriage, when I may have to ask you to undo a belt, or open a door—in other words, when I *let* you love me."

He squeezed her closer to him. "I'll tell you this: When I walked into this house and saw you over there, knowing how you feel about me, well, if I had had fingers at that moment, I'd have snapped them in front of my face several times to see if I were asleep or awake."

Her giggle became a laugh. Startled, she knew maturity was in that laugh. "Nick, did you notice? I laughed at that remark! I burst into laughter when you said that."

"So?"

"That's *it*—it's being able to empathize with you about this handicap of yours. It's being able to laugh or cry with you, free from hang-ups or facades."

He raised interested eyebrows as she went on. "A year ago, I wouldn't have been able to laugh with you over a comment like that. And now, I think it's funny. You meant it to be funny, so immediately I accepted it that way. Working at Davis *did* make a difference."

"Yes, it would have to, I'd say."

"And in Montreux—oh, my darling, at my old school, the Holy Spirit took hold of me and turned my life around."

"I sensed that He must have introduced Himself to you somewhere."

"So I have to take you to Montreux, Nick. You'll have to meet Madame Bouchard and all the others."

"I'd like that. There's a world of wonderful things we'll do together."

"Signor Galdieri wants me back in Turin next August to work on another ballet, but I'll tell him I can't manage—"

"Whoa, take it easy. Why wouldn't you go to Turin? We'll work out something. It'll be tough for me, but I could let you go off for several weeks alone—then I'll join you for a few weeks." ·

"I'm overcome by all this, Nick. Two weeks with you in Turin would be. . ." She groped for words. None seemed appropriate.

"But don't misunderstand me, Claire," he said in a slow, droll manner that suggested a lurking punch line, "I'm not allowing you to be out of my sight for very long. And never forget, lady, when you marry a prison warden, you're shackled for good."

"No parole?" she asked, attempting to keep a straight face.

"From *me?* A parole? Not on your life!"

A Letter To Our Readers

Dear Reader:

In order that we might better contribute to your reading enjoyment, we would appreciate your taking a few minutes to respond to the following questions. We welcome your comments and read each form and letter we receive. When completed, please return to the following:

Rebecca Germany, Fiction Editor
Heartsong Presents
PO Box 719
Uhrichsville, Ohio 44683

1. Did you enjoy reading *A Touching Performance?*
   ☐ Very much. I would like to see more books
     by this author!
   ☐ Moderately
     I would have enjoyed it more if _____

     _____

     _____

2. Are you a member of **Heartsong Presents**? Yes ☐ No ☐
   If no, where did you purchase this book? _____

   _____

3. How would you rate, on a scale from 1 (poor) to 5 (superior), the cover design? _____

4. On a scale from 1 (poor) to 10 (superior), please rate the following elements.

   _____ Heroine   _____ Plot

   _____ Hero   _____ Inspirational theme

   _____ Setting   _____ Secondary characters

5. These characters were special because _____

_____

_____

6. How has this book inspired your life? _____

_____

_____

7. What settings would you like to see covered in future
   Heartsong Presents books? _____

_____

_____

8. What are some inspirational themes you would like to see
   treated in future books? _____

_____

_____

9. Would you be interested in reading other **Heartsong
   Presents** titles?   Yes ❏   No ❏

10. Please check your age range:
    ❏ Under 18   ❏ 18-24   ❏ 25-34
    ❏ 35-45   ❏ 46-55   ❏ Over 55

11. How many hours per week do you read? _____

Name _____

Occupation _____

Address _____

City _____ State _____ Zip _____

down under kind of love

Go down under with a contemporary collection of four complete novels and one novella. Starting in *Search for Tomorrow*, readers will follow Gail as she rebuilds her life after a tragedy takes the ones she loves. In *Search for Yesterday*, they will sympathize with Hilda when she learns she has a father she never knew and strength that had never been tested before. They will root for Beth and Art when they attempt to rebuild a broken body and marriage in *Search for Today*. Then, in the novella, *Search for the Star*, the readers will explore Jean's second chance with an old love. Readers will experience the sights and sounds of Australia as native Australian Mary Hawkins weaves stories of inspirational romance.

paperback, 464 pages, 5 ¾₆" x 8"

❤ ❤ ❤ ❤ ❤ ❤ ❤ ❤ 🖤 ❤ ❤ ❤ ❤ ❤ ❤ ❤ ❤

❤ ❤ ❤ ❤ ❤ ❤ ❤ 🖤 ❤ ❤ ❤ ❤ ❤ ❤ ❤